THE LOST MEN

Ryan Licata

THE LOST MEN

A JOE VELLETRI NOVELLA

Cover design by Hannes Pasqualini

First Edition

ISBN: 979 869 556 1180

Each of us, face to face with others […], is clothed with some sort of dignity, but we know only too well all the unspeakable things that go on in the heart.

– Luigi Pirandello
Six Characters in Search of an Author

One

The drive out to the fields was the carpenter's first time in an American automobile. And the new, shiny red Model T Ford Touring, with its hardy steel frame fitted with plush, black leather seats, brass light features, and wooden interiors, was something to marvel at. Its craftsmanship, a thing of beauty. He remembered reading about the automobile in the newspapers, how the American company claimed to have revolutionised the industry, and there'd be no looking back. The Italian automobile companies were way behind.

Gianni Gambino sat next to the driver. While the man at the wheel kept his eyes on the road, the Sicilian, as usual, had a lot to say. He went on about the Lombardian landscape, how it was too flat for his liking, how he missed the Peloritani Mountains and rugged coastline of Messina. The carpenter listened but took more interest in Gambino's skin, as smooth as sanded wood. He doubted the man had shaved a day in his life.

Gambino repeated that there was a need for tradesmen in New York, and in their line of business carpenters were particularly sought after, saying that with his skill, he'd go far.

Who knew, the Sicilian said, perhaps one day, he himself would be working for Mr. Ford and driving a Model T of his very own. The carpenter raised his eyebrows. Unlikely, he thought, given that the Touring cost around $850, the kind of *denaro* he could only dream of.

When he was told they were taking a drive out to the country to finish their business, he asked where about. Nobody knew Milan better than him. He certainly knew it better than any Sicilians. But Gambino insisted he needn't worry. He even seemed offended. These Sicilians were strange that way. Sensitive. Still, this was a chance he could not turn down. They'd shown him written testimonies from other artisans who'd gone to New York. Their businesses certainly looked legit and it sounded like they made good money. Sure, Milan was his home. He had his friends here. But he also had a wife and children to think about. He wouldn't get another chance like this. He was doing it for his family.

The driver pulled over along the old country road. While the fields – farmlands demarcated with rows of cypress trees, footpaths, and low walls of stone – were familiar, he was surprised he didn't know exactly where they were. The Sicilian's endless talk had distracted him.

Gambino opened his door. 'We'll walk from here,' he said, getting out. 'Giovanni doesn't like to get mud on his Model T.'

The driver swore and restarted the engine. The carpenter hurried out and then watched as the red automobile sped away over a hill towards the darkening horizon.

'Don't worry,' said the Sicilian. 'He'll be back soon.'

They walked up a steep path as the last of the sun sunk ahead of them with reddish hues. He wondered how they'd find their way back to the road after nightfall. He didn't understand why their business couldn't be settled in the city in the way they'd done things before. And at a more reasonable hour.

In the near darkness, the droning cicadas and the distant grunt of pigs unnerved him. At the top of the hill, the stench of manure greeted him along with the sight of a small farmhouse below. The glow of a gas lantern on the porch was the only light. As they descended, horse flies rose from the path and the stench stung his nostrils.

On the porch, in the shadow of the lantern, a man sat sharpening knives. The grating sound of blade on stone was familiar to the carpenter. In the faint light, the man's sculpted beard and moustache against his brown complexion gave him the appearance of a barbarous storybook Turk. He wore a cavalryman's coat from a foreign country. The brass buttons shone like gold coins. The Sicilian greeted the man with a slight nod, a hint of deference. It was the first time Gambino seemed at a loss for words. The man in the shadows did not look up from the sharpening of his knives.

Before entering the house, the carpenter looked down at his mud clogged shoes. He knelt to remove them, but Gambino was quick to stop him.

'We won't be long.'

Again, he wondered why it had been necessary to come so far if their business was merely a formality. He raised his hand to the breast pocket of his coat and felt the bulge of his pocketbook where he kept his passport, documents, and the money. Marianne had tried to dissuade him. It was all they had to live on. But he said that it was an investment, promising that the lean years would be followed by fat ones.

Inside the house, at the end of a passage, men sat at a kitchen table, smoking and drinking. As the carpenter and Gambino entered, some of the men rose and left the room. Remaining at the head of the table sat a well-dressed man he'd never met. His beard was tinged with white and his moustache drooped making his mouth seem small. In front of him was a fedora of black felt and a glass of red wine. On the counter behind him stood an open bottle and a long-barrelled gun.

'Don Vito,' said Gambino, 'I didn't expect you to be here.'

'I'm just passing through. Fetch the book.'

As Gambino left the room, the man at the table regarded the carpenter with stern interest. The Don had a warm face, healthy colour in his cheeks, a man in his fifties enjoying the prime of his life. The air of one who lived comfortably, who was used to fine things. But there was a coldness in his eyes that suggested that these things had come at a cost, perhaps not to himself.

Gambino returned with a ledger and a metal money box. He sat at the table, took out a pen and ink, and opened the book.

'Do you have your documents,' he said.

A feeling of ill-ease came over the carpenter. He could see his wife and children as clearly as if they were in the room: Marianne, that look of concern in her soft brown eyes; his daughter holding her *pelush* bear; and her baby brother, never without the small wooden horse the carpenter himself had carved from black walnut.

'That's the thing,' he said.

The Don leaned forward, knitting his hands.

'Well,' said Gambino, 'out with it.'

The carpenter lowered his eyes and shook his head.

'Come now,' Gambino said nervously, 'let's get this done, so we can get you home to your family.'

The Don glared at the Sicilian, and he shifted in his chair.

'I think I've changed my mind,' said the carpenter.

'We agreed,' said Gambino.

The Don raised his hand for silence. Then he picked up his glass and tilted it slightly. 'New York,' he said, swirling the wine, 'it's an opportunity not everyone has.'

The carpenter nodded.

'Yet you've changed your mind.'

'It's a lot of money,' he said, 'and my wife – '

'Your wife, yes, what better advisor than a wife,' said the Don, smiling. 'Where would we be without our wives?' He looked at Gambino who nodded. 'I myself would not have come this far without mine. But your wife will respect your bold decision and in time will come to thank you.'

The carpenter pressed a hand to his breast pocket. 'She's always wanted to see New York,' he said.

'There you go,' said the Don and raised his glass. '*Salute.*'

But behind the Don, through the red tinged wine glass, the carpenter again saw the long-barrelled gun.

'It's just that the time apart will be difficult,' he said, his hands in fists at his side. 'I'm sorry for the inconvenience, but I wanted to tell you in person. I'm not ungrateful.'

'Of course not,' said the Don.

'I'd like to go home.'

The Don nodded, and Gambino shut the book, left the table, and went down the passage.

'While you wait, why not join me for a glass.'

The Don stood and fetched a wine glass. He covered the gun with a dishrag.

'If it's all the same, I'd like to get back on the road.'

Behind him he heard footsteps. He turned. At the door stood Gambino, his smooth face ashen, and beside him, the dark man from the porch. He brushed back his cavalryman's coat with its shiny brass buttons to reveal a pair of daggers sheathed in the inner linings.

The carpenter looked down again at his muddy shoes. He turned his hands palms up and considered the calluses from years of work. He thought of the dark wooden horse that was probably now in his baby boy's mouth. He slowly lifted his eyes to the Don.

'Please,' he said, 'I want to go home.'

The Don filled his glass, then picked the fedora up from the table and placed it calmly on his head.

'We made an agreement,' he said. 'Let's respect that.'

Two

S itting in the lobby of the *pensione*, the detective drags his large hand down his forehead and presses his thumb and forefinger to his temples. He could do with some more rest, but he's never been able to sleep late. Not even after those long nights of throwing back beer and rye with Antonio Vachris following a rough day on the job. Even then he'd still be up at dawn. Good for him but hell for anyone who crossed his path.

He is greeted warmly by Hao, Xuan's personal secretary, who serves him an americano and the morning paper as he has done ever since his return from Turin a week ago. Just business, apparently. Though he dresses simply in beige or white linen garments, the man's height and prominent cheekbones give him the look of a statesman. He bows, wearing a dignified smile inherited from generations of practiced Chinese sages, then attends to the flowers already arranged in the vases around the room.

The *Milan Gazette* has a tattered look, as if Hao, having read it first, had passed it onto the whole of Chinatown. On occasion, Hao offers him the paper folded open to a particular page. At first this annoyed him, but he soon realized that

Hao intended for him to read articles of interest, ones which enlightened him to the ways of the Chinese community. He appreciates Hao's silent way. He himself has no patience for small talk.

He reads the front page. In Barcelona there is unrest after the prime minister Antonio Maura brought in the Spanish army to combat violent protests following the general strike called by the Solidaridad Obrera, a union of anarchists, socialists, and republicans. According to the article, the trouble started following Maura's call-up of the Cazadores, light infantry reservists, as reinforcements for the ongoing military campaign in Morocco. Many of the reservists are the only breadwinners in poor families with a wage of barely 5 pesetas.

He turns to the national news in which the Italian premier Giovanni Giolitti seems to be jostling support for the upcoming elections wherever he can. Sending out overtures to both the left and the right. What a mess the Kingdom of Italy is in. From north to south nobody can agree on how to govern the country. Will Italians always be an ungovernable people? If they cannot govern their own temperaments, how then can they be governed as a unified state under the same laws?

In the classifieds, he notices an ad for a violin. He thinks back to the night he played outside Adelina's window above the family restaurant on the corner of Lafayette and Spring, another night on which he'd drunk too much and whet his taste for romance. She was delighted, her father infuriated. After his marriage to Adelina, with his courting days behind him, he kept the violin in its case in the closet. But she would take it out and leave it on the mantle, encouraging him to play.

Once she had asked him if he played the violin because of Sherlock Holmes. By that logic, he'd said playfully, he might well also be partial to cocaine. If she could see where he's living now, tucked away amongst brothels and opium dens, she might have wondered then whether his remarks had been in jest.

He folds the newspaper and taps it against his knee. The violin might bring him some comfort. But also invite unwanted reverie. He wonders what Adelina has done with his instrument. Had there been an open casket, would she have placed the violin beside him, so that he could torment the more accomplished musicians biding their time in purgatory?

Coming from her rooms, Xuan greets him with a smile. Her demeanour is as calming as her servant's, and yet her movements are touched with grace, and something else he can't find the words for. Just thinking about it jolts him awake. Quicker than the caffeine.

She goes to the office where she receives her visitors, slowly taking their seats now in the lobby. These men and women intrigue him, coming as they do each day, some bearing gifts while others, with their hats and hearts in their hands, seem to bear their souls, too.

Hao has just brought him a second cup of coffee when two men arrive. He can tell by their expensive suits and silver buckled shoes just what their business might be. It cannot be good. The more brazen of the two men winks at him. He lowers his eyes and sips his coffee. With that absurd baby face of his, Gianni Gambino is easily recognised. One of the few in the Morello gang who he'd managed to extradite back to the Old Country.

Hao greets the men, his expression, at times as soft and malleable as clay, turning now to impenetrable stone. He asks them to raise their hands and he searches inside their coats. From beneath their coats, Hao removes the revolvers from their holsters. They don't make too much fuss giving up their guns. This must be a courtesy visit.

When it comes to other visitors, Xuan conducts all business in her office alone. But now Hao follows the men in and closes the door behind him. Clearly, he knows who can be trusted and who should not be.

The voice of Gambino can be heard, the singsong rise and fall of a man selling what he's come to sell. When he has finished, there is silence. Xuan's soprano voice could raise the roof off heaven, but in matters of business she remains calm.

A moment later, Gambino leaves the office with his crony fast on his heels. The Sicilian's smooth face is now crumpled, denied the milk from the breast that he was clearly intent on sucking. Their guns await them at the entrance.

'You're making a mistake,' says the Sicilian, thrusting his revolver back beneath his coat.

Xuan stands at the threshold of her office. 'The mistake has been yours.'

Gambino brushes the underside of his chin with his hand and leaves. Hao gestures with the slightest of nods in the direction of a man seated in the lobby amongst the others. He rises quickly and follows the two Sicilians out the door.

Xuan welcomes her next client with a smile. She shoots a look across to the detective. A look telling him not to worry. It's that kind of look that worries him the most.

Three

Outside, the young maid Yang has just finished hanging up the linen, white sheets hung on lines drawn across the courtyard. She nods and smiles before returning inside. In the corner of the yard, Chupeng sits against an aged fig tree, his bright eyes shifting up and down the pages of a book resting on his raised knees. At the sound of the detective's steps across the cobbles, the boy looks up.

'I didn't mean to disturb you. What are you reading?'

The boy looks down at the page. 'Pu Songling,' he says quietly. 'Ghost stories.'

'Ah, best read during the day then, eh?'

The boy shrugs.

'May I have a look?'

Chupeng picks up a small leaf from the cobbles, marks his page, and offers him the book with both hands. Considering how precious the book clearly is to the boy, he receives it with due respect. The mauve silk cover is slightly worn with age and handling. Bound in a concertina-like fashion, leporello style, the pages of raw silk are filled with Chinese calligraphy. Some of the passages bear illustrations in black ink. One of these depicts two warrior-like figures, one white, the other black, each drawn with an awful grimace. While the white warrior's tongue hangs from his mouth, the black warrior's eyes bulge menacingly.

'Are these two ghosts?'

Chupeng nods, then stretches out his open hands. The detective returns the book.

'Heibai Wuchang,' the boy says, pointing to the ghastly figures. 'They are the black and white guards of Diyu, the underworld.'

'Heibai Wuchang?' he ventures.

'Xie Bi'an is the white guard and Fan Wu Jiu is the black. They were two constables who died while trying to catch an escaped prisoner.'

The detective hunches beside the boy and looks closer at the page. 'How did they die?'

'Looking for the prisoner. You see, the constables separated and planned to meet beneath the Nantai Bridge before nightfall, that's when the beasts and evil spirits come out from the forest. Wu Jiu arrived first, but while he waited there was a great flood, and he drowned under the bridge.'

'How terrible.'

The boy nods. 'After the flood, Xie Bi'an came to the bridge to find his friend dead and in sadness he hung himself. That is why he is drawn with his tongue this way.' Chupeng opens his mouth and, rolling his eyes back, sticks his own tongue out.

'*Dio mio*,' he says, 'and this is a story for children?'

Chupeng looks at him and frowns, appearing not to understand. 'After death,' the boy continues, 'the Jade Emperor was moved by the actions of the two constables, and he made them the custodians of the dead in their passage to Diyu. When you die, Heibai Wuchang, the white and black ghosts, will be there to meet you.'

'Like the Grim Reaper? *La Morte*?'

The boy nods, his eyes wide and curious, perhaps waiting for further explanation.

With the aid of the knotted fig tree, the detective struggles back to his feet

'Let's hope we never meet any of them, eh?'

The boy stares down at the page a moment. 'They are not bad,' he says, without lifting his eyes. 'They're just dead.'

The detective, feeling a grimace coming to his own face, gives the boy a thoughtful look.

'See you, Chupeng,' he says, then makes his way out the courtyard, avoiding the hanging white sheets.

Along with the sudden pestering thoughts of the afterlife, the muggy weather has brought on the detective's wintry mood. It may be July, but it's the third day in a row of heavy clouds, hiding the true look of summer.

He agreed to meet Alvise Inchiostro at a café inside the Stazione Centrale at ten o'clock. While he doesn't always agree with the journalist's left-wing politics, the man has proven to be reliable and a trustworthy source of information. Having eyes and ears on the streets is something that took him years to build up in the neighbourhoods on the Lower East Side. In Milan, he is still very much a stranger.

On entering the small, crowded café, he tugs down the brim of his derby. Living a clandestine life, with one's eyes to the ground, he's realised how telling a person's shoes are: the workman's boots, the clerk's scuffed imitation leather hidden by a poor polish. And then there are the shoes that speak of money. The men wearing these shoes are two of a kind: those born into money and those born to make it. To tell the difference, one need simply observe how these men walk or even stand. Criminals wear their expensive attire in a way that is too self-aware. Their stance is heavy, as if their consciences weigh them down. And yet they walk with a swagger, as though they are trying to shake that same conscience loose. Women he finds more complicated. A woman's class shines through no matter what she wears. A poor woman who knows how to dress will make her clothes speak for her without betraying her secrets. Such a woman, with an instinct for elegance, will out speak the clothes she wears. Whether she is wearing a rag or a ball gown, a woman who carries herself with confidence will captivate a room.

'Velletri.'

Alvise waves at him from a booth in the corner. Beside him sits a young woman. As he nears the table, she stands politely. She is dressed demurely in a light grey frock. She has soft, brown eyes and ash blonde hair, tied loosely, so that strands fall across her face. Looking around, he takes a seat opposite them and removes his derby, setting it on the seat beside him. On the table are two empty espresso cups.

'Thanks for meeting us,' says Alvise. 'Would you like some coffee?'

'I'd better not. What's this about?' he says, looking at the young woman clutching the handbag in front of her. She holds his gaze fiercely as though she'd made an assumption about him and was now searching for evidence.

'My name is Marianne Greco,' she says with a sense of urgency. 'I need you to find my husband.'

'I don't understand,' he says, already reaching for his derby.

'Signor Inchiostro tells me that you – '

'That I what?' He glares at the journalist who picks up his spoon and digs into the undissolved sugar in his cup.

'All I said was that you might be interested to hear what we have to say.'

The young woman frowns at Alvise and then looks down at her handbag. She opens it and takes out a folded sheet of paper. She is about to hand it to the journalist but then slides it across the table to the detective instead.

As if acting of its own volition, his hand immediately rests on it. Once more, his eyes scan the room. People chatting in other booths and around tables. Commuters and officials coming and going, drinking coffee at the bar. Some pensioners already on white wine.

'You haven't exactly chosen a quiet place to talk,' he says.

'It's neutral territory. That's why it's perfect,' says Alvise. 'I know for a fact that around us are both police and criminals. All of them discussing business, but everything said is caught up in the noise.'

The detective raises his eyebrows. 'What's this then?'

'It's a list of names,' says la Signora Greco.

He unfolds the paper and reads through them.

'The name at the top of the list is my husband. Giacomo Venturini. The others are the husbands of women who've spoken to me.'

'About what? What have these men done?'

'They haven't done anything,' she says in a tempered whisper. 'They've disappeared.'

'Perhaps it'd be better if you tell Signor Velletri what you told me,' says Alvise.

She nods and takes a moment to order her thoughts.

'My husband received an opportunity to travel to New York,' she says. 'He was going to be a part of a new business venture. I was opposed at first, you see, we have two children, a girl and a boy, my boy is only seven months and – '

'What was this business opportunity, Signora Greco?' says the detective.

She places her hands on the edge of the table. 'My husband is a carpenter by trade, the proposal was for him to partner with other tradesmen and refurbish apartments in the expanding Italian community in New York.'

The ever-expanding web of criminals, the detective thinks to himself. 'And who were the people he was dealing with?' he asks.

'She never met them,' says Alvise.

'My husband knew a man on the job who introduced him to another man, a business type.'

'What was the catch?'

'The catch?' she says.

'I'm sure this opportunity came with, well, let's call it a compromise of some sort, am I right?'

'Tell him about the money,' says Alvise.

'The deal was that while the company was set up in New York, Giacomo needed to pay his initial expenses which included the passage from Genoa and his first two weeks of board and lodging which would be arranged before departure. It was a lot of money for us, more than we had in our savings. We had to borrow from our parents, the little that they had.'

'Then you agreed?'

She nods, pushing her coffee cup away. 'Giacomo convinced me. America, you see. We never imagined that we could ever go, but we have heard how it is over there, how people can prosper.'

The detective thinks of the slums of the Lower East Side where the only thing prospering is the stench of the slops thrown from tenement windows.

'So what happened?'

'Giacomo was told to prepare his travel documents, his passport as well as the birth certificate that the immigration officers needed. And the money. On previous occasions he met the men during the day, but the night of his disappearance he was picked up in the early evening. That was the last I saw of him.'

Again, he reads the list of names. 'And you say the wives of these men have similar stories?'

'Yes, the women all told me that their husbands were given job opportunities in New York. They sailed from Genoa and have not been heard from since.'

The detective frowns. He has lost count of the Italian men who have arrived in New York with the promise of sending for their wives and children only to take up with other women or die before they get the chance.

'How long has it been since your husband's departure?'

'He didn't depart, he's missing,' she says, gripping her handbag. 'It's been almost a week today.'

'You insist he's disappeared?'

'I'm not insisting, I know.'

'The ship takes at least two weeks.'

'But he wasn't departing, I mean, he didn't just leave without saying goodbye. He was just going to talk.'

'With his travel documents and your money,' he says, eyeing Alvise.

'No,' says la Signora Greco, raising her voice, attracting some attention from customers nearby. 'You're not listening.'

Alvise puts a hand on her shoulder.

'Velletri,' says the journalist, 'I think there is more to this.'

'Perhaps,' says the detective, turning the list over in his hands. 'Forgive me, but we all know men and when they disappear, well, we know what men are like.'

'That's not my husband,' says la Signora Greco, her eyes fierce, glaring first at the detective and then at Alvise.

'What we're hoping is,' says Alvise, 'well, if you could just take this list and look into it. Perhaps you have people in New York. They might know something.'

19

He has people, sure, but those people think he's pushing up daisies. He raps a knuckle on the table. There is one lifeline between the living and the dead. But the less he gets involved the better.

'If it's a question of money,' says la Signora Greco. She quickly sweeps the room with her eyes then takes an envelope from her handbag. 'The others and I have put together what we can.'

He raises a hand. 'Let's wait and see,' he says. 'Do you have a photograph of your husband, Signora?'

Her brown eyes are softened even more by tears which she quickly wipes away with the back of her hand. She returns the money to her handbag and takes out a small photograph. 'This was taken during his military service,' she says, 'but it's quite recent.'

The man in the picture is dressed smartly in uniform and has an amiable face, with large, expressive eyes, almost as warm and as sensitive as his wife's. The detective folds the list and slips it together with the picture into his coat pocket.

'I shall see what I can do, Signora.' He puts on his derby, lowers the brim, and slides out the booth. The young woman stands, and he smiles as warmly as he can, before glaring at Alvise who shies away, scratching deeper into the bottom of the cup with his spoon.

As the detective waits in the queue at the post office, the meeting with la Signora Greco weighs on his mind. While he has kept minimal contact with Sergeant Antonio Vachris, it is reassuring knowing that his old partner and friend is there for his wife and daughter. Adelina has her brother and father, but Vachris can be relied upon should she be in danger. His decision to have Adelina believe he is dead, and to have others believe it, is for his family's safety. But his conscience tells him that only a bad man abandons a wife and child. What kind of man lets the woman he loves believe that he is dead? Allows his own daughter to grow up without a father? Perhaps one day he can make things right. For now, he is making them safe. He needs to keep telling himself that.

He takes the list of men from his pocket. How many Joe Petrosinos are on this list? He knows personally men who began families in New York while their families back in Italy starved. In the beginning, they are sent money, but in time they are abandoned. Supporting one family is hard enough in the slums of Little Italy.

He wires a telegram to Vachris in New York with the names of the five men. At the end of it, he includes one more: Giuseppe Velletri.

Four

In the middle of the night, he wakes up to the slamming of doors, a rush of voices back and forth. He opens the shutters and peers down into the courtyard. Xuan dressed in her nightgown, her hair worn in a single plait, listens to a small gathering of Chinese who, one at a time, appear to be relaying messages to her. Meanwhile, beside her, Hao attends to a group of armed men who then hurry out into the night. He sees the boy Chupeng come running. He delivers a written note, before he too is sent back out. Xuan looks up at him, but her expression renders him no more significant than the moss-covered eaves beneath his window.

He lies down again and shuts his eyes. But the coming and going of messengers and the pressing voice of Xuan, their commander, won't let him sleep. He pulls on his trousers and a collarless shirt and goes downstairs.

Hao sees him first and raises a gentle but warning hand.

'It's OK, Hao,' says Xuan.

'What's happened?' he asks.

Just then, an elderly shopkeeper stumbles into the courtyard, bleeding from a cut on his head, his hair wet with blood.

'A declaration of war,' Xuan says, turning towards the injured man.

One of the maids quickly attends to the shopkeeper, applying a cloth to his head, speaking softly to him. He nods and holds the cloth in place. When calmer, he tells his story to Xuan. She listens, and when she replies the old man seems pleased with her answer. He is led away, and she sends another of her foot soldiers running from the courtyard.

'The men who came to see me yesterday are responsible for this,' she says, looking up at the windows that surround them.

'Responsible?'

'They have attacked stores in the quarter. Many have had their windows broken, their merchandise damaged or stolen. Some of the owners have been beaten.'

'And you are sure that it was the men from yesterday?'

She faces him with the indulgent look of a mother whose child has asked a silly question.

'What will you do?' he asks.

'That is not your concern.'

'You need to be careful,' he says. 'These men are not shy to kill.'

Hao and Xuan exchange glances. 'You're right,' she says. 'And such men need to learn their place.'

'I just don't want you to invite any unnecessary trouble.'

She regards him closely, her head cocked slightly, and he finds himself raising a hand to the exposed scar on his neck.

'Best you get some sleep, Joe. I'm sorry to have woken you.' She turns from him and attends to yet another messenger. Hao, with a bow, bids him good night.

He returns to bed, but sleep won't come. Instead, in wakeful dreams, he fights off shapes of black fedoras, *luparas*, bulging eyed corpses. And when sleep is finally about to settle on him, the light-footed steps of the maids up and down the corridor tell him that it's morning.

He opens the shutters. The clouds are darker than yesterday. The humid air already sticks to his skin. From the bed, he pulls off the sheets damp with sweat and leaves them outside the door.

Downstairs there is no sign of Hao or Xuan. The *Milan Gazette* lies on the lounge table. He skims the front page. The conflict in Barcelona has spilt out into other parts of Catalonia. Workers and rioters have taken control of the city centre, halting trains and even overturning trams. The presence of Spanish soldiers has escalated, as has the loss of civilian lives. In the local news, there are the usual political debates surrounding Giolitti and the election. There is no mention of Chinatown.

The moment he leaves the quiet haven of the *pensione's* leafy courtyard, he faces the aftermath of last night's tumult. Ruined goods, busted furniture, broken glass. The damage stretches across every street he walks down. Via Paolo Sarpi is the worst hit. Chinese shop owners are hard at work sweeping up the glass from the pavements. A woman helps a man secure wooden panels to the front of their grocery store. She regards the detective suspiciously before her husband, glancing back, says something to her, and only then does she greet him with a friendly look.

'Velletri? What time do you call this?' says Finn, ambling up the street with two brushes tucked awkwardly under his arm and a heavy bucket in each hand.

'Early for you too, isn't it?'

'Help me out here,' says the Irishman, passing the detective one of the buckets filled with white paint.

'Business that bad, eh?'

Finn attempts a smile. 'Take a look around you. We got the same treatment. Our bar was vandalised.'

'But you're not – '

'Chinese?' he says, tugging on his red beard. 'We might as well be as far as those hoodlums are concerned.'

Outside the bar, Finn's wife Ofelia uses a hard brush to scrub away the slogans written in black paint across the wall. The familiar open palmed hands and skulls, like children's scribbles, used by the Black Hand and other thugs affiliated with them. He greets Ofelia. She drops the brush and knits her fingers in her curly hair, bunched up on her head and tied loosely. Her usual friendly, good-humoured talk is all bound up inside of her.

'I'm sorry, Joe,' she says. 'It's too much for me.'

Finn puts his arms around her. 'We're gonna have to paint this wall. It'll take a few coats.'

The detective goes into the bar.

Finn calls after him, 'We're not open, old boy.'

He takes off his overcoat and hat, then rolls up his sleeves and comes out again. 'Let's get this done,' he says, picking up a hard brush.

Once the repairs are done on the bar, they eat the food the Chinese restaurants have provided during the course of the morning. Finn in return has offered a glass of beer to anyone who will take it. After lunch, they again set to work, helping their neighbours board up broken windows and scrub off or paint over the slogans and marks of the Black Hand. Only a few stores on Via Paolo Sarpi have been spared.

An elderly Italian man wearing pressed linen slacks, an immaculate white shirt, and braces, walks casually up the street smoking a fat, expensive cigar. He appears to take in the damage in a disinterested sweep of his eyes shadowed by bushy eyebrows. On noticing the man, the Chinese store owners clip their lively chatter. While some turn their heads away, others glare as he passes.

'What gives?' asks the detective, wiping a forearm across his brow.

Ofelia waits for the man to go farther up the street before replying. 'That's Domenico Tagliatore,' she says. 'He owns the barbershop.'

The detective watches the man with interest. His slow gait seems tempered by arrogance rather than by age.

'He's known as the Don of Chinatown in the Italian quarter,' says Finn. 'Of course, the barbershop wasn't touched last night. It isn't under Madam Xuan's protection.'

'Her protection? Do you pay her?'

'Most of the businesses in the quarter are under her mandate, which means that we contribute to a common fund.'

'And how are these funds used?'

'A portion goes to paying for the Spring Festival.'

'Chinese New Year? Isn't that paid for by Milan's city council. The people in this quarter pay taxes, surely – '

Ofelia shakes her head. 'The city council doesn't recognise the Chinese holidays. An offering from the funds means that certain regulations are ignored during the festival.'

'You mean the council is paid off?'

'I suppose you could call it that. The funds are also used as insurance.'

'So it'll pay for these damages?'

'That's the idea. The Chinese businesses survive partly because of Madam Xuan's influence, but also because of the Chinese citizen's commitment to each other. Chinese buy from other Chinese. But the few Italian owned businesses don't do so well, especially if they don't agree to Madam Xuan's terms.'

'The only ones to survive are those carried by organised crime,' adds Finn. 'Even then, there is no guarantee. They bleed you dry.'

Literally, the detective thinks.

The barber turns on his heels and looks back down the street. He takes the thick cigar from his mouth and taps ash from the tip.

'Our Don here seems to be doing alright.'

'That's because he's a boss, at least, we think so.'

'We seldom see customers going into the barbershop,' Ofelia explains. 'Nobody from around here, and yet he's been in business longer than anyone.'

'My guess is that his shop is a front for something else,' says Finn.

'Have you ever been approached by the Friends?'

'Approached? You mean threatened?' says Finn. 'Not directly. Men come to the bar and have a drink and try the food, but also flex their muscles, show their guns, and then leave.'

'We know they're evaluating how we do business,' says Ofelia. 'And letting us know that they're around.'

'But they've never made an offer,' says Finn. 'There was an understanding of sorts when Giovanni Pappalardo was around. He may not have been a boss, but he definitely had some say on how things were being run. Businesses under Madam Xuan's protection were not to be touched.'

The detective shuts his eyes. Just hearing the name Pappalardo causes his hands to clench into fists. The recent memory of the Levitas and their son Davide still tightens his heart. The death of the men responsible is no consolation.

'But now that Pappalardo's gone,' continues Finn, 'there seems to be a lot more Sicilian muscle in this quarter.'

'Rather the enemy you know,' says the detective, watching as the barber disappears around the next corner, leaving behind a pungent ghost of cigar smoke that wafts up into the already grey air.

'We'll see,' Ofelia says. She leans her head on Finn's chest, and he puts his arms around her.

The detective walks back towards the *pensione*, weary from the day's toil but satisfied to see the community pull together. He could not imagine anything similar happening on the Lower East Side, where one's neighbours may have been generous in times of hardship, but if those hardships were brought on by the Friends, then people didn't get involved. For fear of the repercussions.

The *pensione* is strangely quiet. At this hour, there is usually music, *her* music, the arias whose mysterious cadence hold him entranced. Also, the vases remain empty. Sapping the room of its former colour and charm. The door to Xuan's rooms is closed, locking in a silence that too hangs with a foreboding that he knows can come to no good.

In his room, he pulls the shutters on the ever-gloomier clouds. How much will it take before the storm breaks?

Five

He is awoken in the night by tapping outside his window. He sighs, thinking that finally the rain has come. But the drops, heavy as hailstones, fall few and far between. On opening the shutters, a pebble hits him in the chest. Down in the courtyard, Chupeng stands, his arm drawn back, ready to let fly another stone. Seeing the detective, the boy puts a finger to his lips and waves for him to come down.

Downstairs, the large door to the courtyard is locked. The ground floor windows are barred from the outside. He goes in search of Yang or one of the other maids. But nobody is around. He runs back up to his room. He peers again into the courtyard, but Chupeng has disappeared. He wants to call out his name, but then thinks it better to heed the boy's warning. Perhaps silence now is an ally.

He looks down at the tiled roofs that taper towards the cobblestones below. He crosses himself and climbs out onto the window ledge. In the far end of the courtyard, from behind one of the old fig trees, Chupeng appears out of the shadows. The detective turns his body cautiously and, holding on to the ledge, lowers himself down until his feet touch the narrow roof below. He curses his short legs. He sits down on the moss covered tiles and edges his way forward on his bottom. Again he manoeuvrers his body 'round and, clinging to the branch of a fig tree, he dangles, then drops to solid ground. Chupeng is there to greet him, smiling and clapping silently.

'Where to?' whispers the detective.

Chupeng reaches up to his shoulder and brushes off some dirt from his coat. Satisfied, the boy runs swiftly out the courtyard, with the detective doing his best to keep up.

Arriving at Via Alessandro Volta, the unwritten border between the Chinese and Italian quarters, Chupeng stops at the corner of an unlit alley. Across the street, beneath a streetlamp, police officers stand closely together. Amongst them, he makes out the broad-shouldered figure of Chief Inspector Cattaneo and his right-hand man, Sergeant Bruno. The chief warns off Alvise, who backs away with his camera aimed up at one of the lampposts. It's only then that the detective sees what the fuss is about. From the post hangs a body. A glint of light catches the buckle of the dead man's shoes.

Alvise sees the detective and, with a quick glance at the officers, darts across the street.

'Good,' says the journalist. 'You came.'

A small hand emerges from the alley, palm out.

'Right,' says Alvise, reaching into his trouser pocket.

He digs out a few coins and gives them to Chupeng. The boy counts the money, then bows to the two men, and disappears, his footstep tapping like Morse code back through the Chinese quarter.

'What was that about?' says the detective.

'Our little messenger seems to have wisened up to the ways of the world,' says Alvise. 'You're not an easy man to find, Velletri.'

'It wasn't exactly easy to get away.'

'Sorry to get you out of bed.' He points to the man hung up from the lamppost. 'Do you recognise him?'

The detective nods, pulling the collar of his coat close against the evening chill. 'Let's go have a closer look.'

He takes a step forward only for Alvise to hold him back by the arm.

'Hang on,' he says. 'You may want to rethink going over there. The chief seems to be out for blood.'

'I'm sure one corpse is enough for this evening.'

'It's your funeral.'

What's one more? the detective thinks.

At their approach, the chief turns and exhales heavily. '*Santo cielo*, I was hoping you'd left town, but then I get a call out at this godforsaken hour to see this year's Christmas lights strung up early.'

'Good evening to you, too, Chief Inspector.'

'If this isn't your handywork, I'll put it down to Sicilian internal affairs.'

The detective grunts and takes a Toscano cigar from his pocket. 'I know who he is, if you're interested – '

'Oh, I'm always interested in what you have to say. I'd just prefer to hear it before someone gets killed.'

'His name's Gianni Gambino,' the detective says quietly, turning the cigar between his thumb and forefinger.

As if this introduction to the deceased called for some formal acknowledgement, the chief inspector looks up at the corpse, shielding his eyes from the light of the lamp. 'Gambino, eh? Well, he's in God's hands now.'

'I doubt that. He was a thug, a member of the Morello gang. Looks to me like he got what he deserved. Maybe even a little less.'

'A New Yorker's idea of justice, is it?'

'New York?' says an officious little man, emerging from the automobile, holding a clipboard against his chest. 'That's somewhat out of your jurisdiction, Chief Inspector.'

Cattaneo clears his throat. 'This is Gilberto Scalisi,' he says, touching his brow as though he feels a headache coming on. 'He's here from Rome.'

'And you are?' says the official, burrowing his narrow, close-set eyes into the detective.

'Giuseppe Velletri,' he says, introducing himself. The man from Rome, pursing his thin lips, lowers his clipboard, lifts a page, and appears to study his notes.

The chief inspector eyes the official's reaction. 'Signor Velletri works as, well, let's say, a consultant, off the books, so to speak.'

'Consulting in what exactly?' asks Scalisi.

'Night-time fiascos,' says Cattaneo, losing his patience.

Scalisi asks no more questions, but, taking a pencil from behind a pointy ear, he scratches a note on his clipboard. The detective bites down on his cigar, letting loose a flurry of tobacco to chew on.

'Alright, the show's over,' says Cattaneo. 'Bring him down boys, slowly.'

One of the chief's men, a young officer, hoists a stepladder up against the post and scampers up. His uniform looks brand-new. Sergeant Bruno assists him, holding the dead man's feet, while the youngster attempts to untie the rope.

'Can't loosen this knot, Chief Inspector.'

'Here,' says Cattaneo, passing the young man his army issue knife, 'cut the rope but don't damage the knot. Forensics may be able to find something.'

The rope is cut, and the corpse is slowly lowered to the street.

Gambino's once smooth, tanned face appears aged, wrinkled and whiter than the paving stones he lies on. The rope tied around his neck runs down to his bound hands through a complex series of knots.

'I've never seen anything like this,' says Cattaneo, brushing a hand back across his cropped hair.

The detective grinds the tobacco with his teeth. There isn't much he hasn't seen.

Everyone steps aside as two men from the coroner office, Ciccio and Mignon, arrive on the scene. Mignon, wearing white cotton gloves, kneels beside the body and does a brisk examination. 'His left shoulder's dislocated,' he says.

'That might explain these knots,' says the inspector. 'I'm guessing the more he struggled the more painful it became.'

'Let's get him on to the stretcher,' says Ciccio, about to head back to the coroner wagon.

'Wait,' says Mignon, moving his forefinger along the neck of the corpse. 'This is unusual.' He rapidly unbuttons Gambino's shirt, soiled with dried blood and what appears to be the bile from an empty stomach.

'*Dio mio*,' cries Mignon.

The others lean closer.

'*Che impressione*,' says Alvise, readying his camera. Mignon obliges by opening the dead man's shirt fully, exposing a series of intricately carved Chinese characters on his chest. The man from Rome averts his eyes and raises a handkerchief over his mouth and nose.

Ciccio crouches beside Mignon. 'The wounds seem to have been treated with alcohol,' he says, making notes.

Alvise snaps a picture. The flashing bulb light irritates the chief, jolting him from his thoughts.

'Inchiostro,' he says, 'you're not to publish that, *hai capito*?'

Alvise sighs, adjusting his flat cap.

'*Hai capito, sì o no*?' barks the chief, waving a fist.

'*Sì, ho capi.*'

'Well,' says Cattaneo, turning to the detective. 'If there was any doubt as to who is responsible, we have our answer in writing.'

'I doubt it's a confession,' says the man from Rome, his voice muffled behind his handkerchief. A hint of a smug smile in his narrow, shifty eyes.

Cattaneo ignores the official and, looking at the corpse, mutters to himself. 'Officer Esposito,' he says, 'find me someone who can decipher Chinese.'

The young officer salutes and slides down the ladder.

The detective chews noisily on the end of the cigar, bits of tobacco sticking to his tongue.

'Something you'd like to say, Velletri,' says Cattaneo.

He takes the cigar from his mouth and looks over his shoulder. The body lies outside the Chinese quarter. This is a clear response to the Sicilians running the other side. He spits out a soggy mess of tobacco. 'You better have empty pallets in your morgue, Chief Inspector,' he says. 'You're going to need them.'

Six

The detective, slowly making his way back to bed, turns things over in his mind. Given Gambino's past, the man's death concerns him more than it should. The brutality of it clashes with his growing sentiments for Xuan and her household. It's a scab covered wound that's beginning to itch. He knows what scratching brings.

Out of the corner of his eye, he catches a glimpse of the journalist heading downtown. Dashing off no doubt to get his pictures and article to print in time for the morning paper.

The journalist reappears and waits at the next corner.

'Are you lost?' says the detective.

'I didn't want the chief to see us talking.'

'Not good for business, eh?'

'He doesn't seem to like you much.'

'I hadn't noticed. He's obviously threatened by my charming personality.'

'Nothing to do with your past then, no?'

The detective stops, throwing what's left of his cigar into an open dumpster. 'What he knows or doesn't know about me isn't your concern.'

'Maybe.'

'Not maybe, it's categorically so.'

'I just thought that if we are going to work together, then you should be straight with me. Who do you work for?'

'It's like you said yourself, we are on the same side, but the less you know about me, the safer we'll both be. Satisfied?'

Alvise adjust his flat cap and looks down the street. 'How about I buy you a drink?'

'You think a little liquor is going to loosen my tongue? The only thing you're going to loosen is my temper.'

'I get it. I just thought we could discuss the missing men.'

'I haven't heard anything yet.'

'I've been doing a little digging on my own. I know a bar that's open.'

'At this time of night?' The detective's interest is piqued, along with his thirst. 'I guess your line of work has its perks.'

'The best kept secret in Milan.'

'Lead the way.'

Away from the glow of the city centre, they walk further into the Chinese quarter, weaving down alleys that come out into hidden courtyards, which then lead to more side streets. The detective looks around, trying to find his bearings. While the courtyards are occasionally lit by lamps burning in windows, the alleys are increasingly dark as they walk on, descending into an ever more confined maze.

'You seem to know your way around.'

'As you said, being a journalist has its advantages. Also, the people I see are not the types who like to be seen.'

'If you want to catch a rat, you have to find its hole, right?'

'I'm not only in the business of rats, Velletri. I'm out for rubies, too.'

Suddenly, they burst through the darkness into a court-yard brightly lit with red paper lanterns. Flowering ivy twists its way through elaborate wrought iron balconies and along the sides of stone walls. Entering a narrow, open door, they follow the warm glow of smaller hanging lanterns down a corridor. Dark music surrounds them, like the hum of a train rising from the belly of the earth.

The passage is lined on either side with several arched doorways leading to chambers concealed behind heavy, velvet curtains. The sound of feminine laughter touches the detective's ears, stirring in him tender memories. At the end of the corridor, a red tasselled curtain parts soundlessly.

'Alvise, *amore*,' says a Chinese woman in a long, black, lowcut dress. 'Why haven't you come to see me?'

'My apologies, Madam Jing,' he says, kissing the woman's cheeks. 'I've been busy.'

She takes Alvise by the hand and invites them inside a dimly lit, low-ceilinged lounge bar decorated with cushioned booths. At the far end of the room is a polished wooden stage before a red velvet curtain. More quiet feminine laughter lies behind it. The laughter seems to rise, as if from beneath the sea. No sooner does it surface, than it is swept away by a rush of waves.

'And who's your friend,' says their host, coming up to him. While her rich timbre voice and the crow's feet at the corners of her eyes suggest that she is in her fifties, she possesses the playfulness of a youthful temptress. The art of seduction is also the art of concealment. Her face is so close to his that he can smell her perfume, see the fine dustings of gold powder on her skin. '*Posso?*' *May I?* she says, slipping his hat from his head. '*Quanto sei carino, ometto. Come ti chiami?*'

'Madam Jing, this is Giuseppe Velletri,' says Alvise, his smile suggesting complicity in the detective's discomfort at the hands of this woman.

'*Piacere,*' she says. '*Ma che ti è successo?*' *What's happened to you?* She runs her forefinger down the length of the scar on his cheek. He grabs her hand and pulls it away from his face.

She is not alarmed by his aggression. She smiles calmly and places his hat on the bar counter. He lets go of her hand and allows her to remove his coat.

'Thank you,' he says.

'How about something to drink?' She goes behind the well-stocked bar and takes down a bottle. 'This was a gift from a Scot. Would you believe the man was wearing one of those skirts.'

'I believe they're called kilts,' says Alvise.

'Yes, that's what he said, a kilt. The girls loved it. Oh, he was very popular with them.'

'I see you're busy tonight?' says Alvise.

The detective looks around at all the empty booths, and again his curiosity is pulled towards what lies behind the velvet curtain. And what unfolds on the stage.

'Politicians from Rome are here for the weekend,' says Madam Jing. 'All the girls are busy.' She looks intently at the detective, setting a tumbler of neat whisky in front of him.

'Of course, I'm always at the disposal of newcomers, my treat.'

The detective takes the glass and, averting his eyes from the woman's intense gaze, whiffs the scotch. The aged barrel scent burns his nostrils and clears his head.

She smiles at him and then serves Alvise. 'Your friend's terribly shy.'

'He is,' says Alvise, shrugging. 'He just needs warming up.'

The detective groans, then takes his drink and sits at one of the booths. Alvise joins him, sitting opposite. Madam Jing stays behind the bar. Her eyes do not leave him.

'I'd say you've made quite an impression on the lady of the house.'

'That's the second time this evening you've underestimated my charm,' says the detective, raising his glass. '*Salute.*'

The whisky goes down finer than the barrel rot he used to drink in the dives back home. Judging by the selection of bottles behind the bar, each of the highest quality liquor, the house must be frequented by clientele with money, and a taste for what it can buy.

'So, let's hear it,' says the detective.

'Right,' says Alvise. 'I didn't want to mention it yesterday in front of la Signora Greco, but I've a good source of information. A connection with the trains. A guy named Fabio Martinelli who works for Ferrovie dello Stato. His department is a branch of the government's security sector. He keeps an eye on who's buying tickets, that is, who's going where and when. He receives lists each day from the government, partly to make sure that the dignitaries and diplomats entering the country are safe but also not going places they're not supposed to.'

'A spy?'

'He'd prefer to think of himself as a gate watcher. I've given Martinelli the list of the men. He's checked the records of people travelling over the last month, but they're not kept for longer than that. Also, he has no immediate access to maritime journeys. It doesn't fall under his domain. Anyway, he's keeping an eye on things for me. In the meantime, I did some checking up on the men myself, and they're all clean.'

'You mean, *cleaned*.'

'I don't think so. Not only are there no police files, but I looked into their school records, and these men are all *liceo* graduates.

The detective leans his weight on the table. 'Does that impress you?'

'A little, I mean, that's some achievement. Only one in ten men get above middle school education in this country.'

'So they're smart, that doesn't mean they're moral.'

Alvise shakes his head and peers down at his glass. 'You still think these men have just gone off and abandoned their wives?'

'I'm just being realistic. You try travelling across an ocean, start a new life for yourself in a country where you don't speak the language and you're not welcome, it isn't easy.'

'Is that your story?'

'Stop fishing, you're only going to come up with a boot and a kick in the pants.'

Alvise raises his eyebrows. '*Vabbè*, all I'm saying is that these men don't seem like they're the types to get involved in anything.'

'So why did they?'

He shrugs. 'Like many others, they were sold a dream.'

'There has to be more to it. We need to speak to their wives.'

'They won't talk. They're scared.'

'What about la Signora Greco? She doesn't seem scared to me.'

'She's definitely got fight in her. She came directly to my office. She reads my articles in the *Gazette*, apparently. I'd never thought my readers might be women.'

'You surprise me, Alvise. In my experience women are better readers than men, well, more astute anyway.'

The journalist raises his eyebrows with a smirk. 'What else do you know about women? I saw how well you handled that situation just now.' He cocks his head in the direction of their host, who now sits gazing at the detective's hat at the end of the bar.

'I know enough, *ragazzino*.' He taps his fingers on the table and then throws back the rest of the scotch. 'Anyway, I should have a reply from my contact in New York by tomorrow. Then I'll speak to la Signora Greco.'

Alvise turns his glass slowly. 'Tell me about your contact.'

'He's a lot like me. He doesn't like being spoken about.'

'Or spoken to,' says the journalist, shaking his head.

'How about you drink up and get me out of this den? Your lady friend won't stop undressing me with her eyes, and she seems awfully fond of my hat.'

The journalist leans closer. 'The reimagining of the beloved,' he says. 'It's one of the lessons in the art of seduction.'

'Well, ask her if she'd mind imagining me a fast way back to bed.'

'Oh, I'm sure she'd oblige.'

'I meant alone.'

They finish their drinks, and the detective retrieves his coat. But before he can get to his hat, Madam Jing snatches it. She comes round the bar, walking slowly up to him. Then, kissing his forehead, she positions his hat carefully on his head.

'Come back soon,' she says. 'I'll be waiting.'

Seven

Ismael Martinez Ruiz finds the quiet of early mornings more restorative than a night's rest. Years of sleeping rough have conditioned his body. He cannot bear soft mattresses and prefers to make his bed on the floor. He rolls off the rug, does his routine fifty push-ups and a series of stretches, then pulls on his boots.

Out on the porch, he takes papers and tobacco from his pouch and rolls a cigarette. With the others asleep, it is only at this hour that he is sure to find the solitude he needs.

The rising sun hastens the flight of the night's beasts. He takes solace in witnessing their retreat. A fox darts from behind the barn to the shelter of a nearby cluster of shrubs. It has not been fooled by Di Primo's flimsy traps. But neither has its hunt for chickens been successful. Still, he admires the fox, a cunning predator that bides its time.

He twists his moustache and smokes. The night sky slowly lifts, a thin crack of sunlight outlining the distant hills beneath the heavy grey cloud. The stark band of light reminds him of the fires that swept across the fields the night the rebels retreated into the Cuban jungle, burning the crops behind them.

He removes the daggers from the leather sheaths sewn into the linings of his coat. Toledo daggers, marked by the two eagles' heads in opposite directions at the hilt, crafted by his own blood – *su padre*, a respected figure in the Toledo guild of smiths. In all his years of war, never had he come across anything superior to Toledo steel. Not by chance had Toledo swords been used by the armies of Hannibal and the Roman legions after them.

He takes out the whetting stone and sharpens the blades. The edges glimmer as he holds each dagger up in turn to the light. The left side of his mouth quivers. His father's gift to him on the day he left to join the Spanish campaign in Cuba had been auspicious. As if he'd sensed his betrayal. How many rebels had he killed before he came to admire their courage? So few against so many, fighting for their freedom from a foreign oppressor. Like those few Spartans against the superior Persian army.

He'd sailed to Cuba under the leadership of Arsenio Martinez Campos, only to end up fighting alongside the Cubans against Campos's successor Valeriano Weyler. By the time the Americans entered the war, he was fighting for whomever paid the highest. He was his own leader. And ruthless.

He remembers the night that Cuban *perro* Alfonso made the mistake of trying to steal a ration of chorizo from under him. He'd slit the man's throat without a thought. Alfonso's son witnessed it all. The boy knelt at his dead father's side. Then he looked Ruiz in the eyes and said, without fear, '*No eres nada mas que un asesino.*'

That's when he'd had the epiphany. The boy was right. *Nada mas que un asesino.* It was a calling. Perhaps his father had known it all along. His gift of daggers instead of the coveted sword was a gesture of love. For who knows a son better than his father? For his part in this realisation, he had shown mercy to Alfonso's boy. He left the rebel camp at dawn, retreating along with the other beasts of the night.

The Americans had shown their gratitude by giving him passage to America. In New York, he'd met the Don. It was unlike the Sicilians to recruit outsiders, men who were not Sicilian, not even Italian, to do their killing. But the Don was a man of honour, a man whose love for respect and other men's fear was far stronger than the love of money. Ruiz respected that. A man after his own heart. Money was easy to get, but a man's fear was something that money could not buy. The Don recognised his talent and knew that he was the assassin that men feared most.

He polishes his daggers and returns them to the sheaths inside his coat. It's time for him to do what is expected of him, what he does best. The death of Gambino had made an impression on him. He'd seen the Sicilian's body with his own eyes. Strung up like a rabbit, a reminder of the man's worth carved into his chest. He admired the work of the Chinese masters. He too considered himself an artist, and he was not too proud to learn from the killing methods of others. But the death of one of the Don's men called for vengeance. It was the Sicilian way. The way of war. Simply, the way of men. Now it was his turn. He would make his mark and make it well.

Eight

The next morning, despite his late night, the detective wakes up at dawn. On returning home, he'd been lucky to find Hao attending the gate to the courtyard. No words had passed between them as he entered the *pensione* and plodded up to his room.

Now, in the lobby, serving him coffee and the *Gazette*, Hao asks him nothing about his nocturnal affairs or how he'd got out. The detective returns the favour by not inquiring why there'd been the need to escape in the first place.

The vases remain empty, and still there is no sign of Xuan. He looks at the window to her office, but the venetian blinds are drawn. Nobody is waiting to see her. With these austerity measures in place, it certainly feels like there's a war on.

On the front page, the reportage of more civilian deaths in Catalonia sits in contrast to the main item of local news. The grainy picture of the police looking up at a shadowy figure hanging from a lamppost seems almost comical. A caricature of police bafflement. And it's only the beginning. Although no credit is given to the photographer, he knows who took the picture. He'd underestimated the journalist's efficiency. Alvise's accompanying article is well-written, presenting the facts of which there are few: the location of the crime, the victim's name, the apparent cause of death. The picture itself should make this clear, but the autopsy report might reveal an alternative explanation. While there is mention of the knife wounds, Alvise has chosen not to reveal their specific nature. Perhaps wisely, he doesn't want to incite animosity towards the Chinese community. It'll inevitably come from Gambino's so-called Friends.

He is impatient to get down to the post office, but he quickly turns to the classifieds and checks to see if the violin is still for sale. It isn't. He tips the rest of the coffee down his throat. Perhaps it's for the best.

Setting down his cup, he catches a glimpse of Xuan peering out at him from the raised blinds in her office. Has she been there all along? He waves and she lowers her gaze and shuts the blinds once again.

Late morning is the busiest time at the post office. A senior postal clerk recognises him standing in the queue and ushers him aside.

'Signor Velletri? You've received an urgent dispatch from the U.S. You're requested to make a long-distance call. Transatlantic connections are still very unreliable, in experimental stages, really. But we've made arrangements for you.'

The man leads him to a small office with an abnormally large switchboard. A microphone is set before him and he is connected by an operator. The line is an angry swarm of wasps. Eventually, on the other side, as the static dissipates, he makes out a familiar voice.

'Joe? Is that you?'

There is a delay, but otherwise he can hear Vachris clearly.

'It's good to hear your voice, Antonio.'

'It certainly is, Joe. Look this line is unstable, also best not to raise suspicion, so I'll have to make this brief.'

'Yes, of course. I'm listening.'

'I've looked into the five names. We have records for four of the men. Since their arrival all of them have been picked up at least once for shady dealings, one is even in custody as we speak, the others are out on bail. The usual misdemeanours we expect from our *mafiosi* friends. Theft, assault, extortion.'

'What about the fifth name, Giacomo Venturini?'

'No record of him. Nothing. Which means he hasn't arrived. Of course, he may be on the next ship.'

'Anything else?'

'The books held at Ellis Island say all four men arrived with substantial funds. Nothing overly suspicious, but a lot more than is usual. It didn't occur to the officials to report it, as the men had work contracts already in place and were registered as being on official business. These are the types that the officials like dealing with, because they're not expecting a handout from the American tax-payers' money, and they're more likely to offer generous bribes, in cash, which you well know our upstanding officials are happy to accept.'

The static surfaces again, followed by a high-pitched ringing. Then, quiet.

'Vachris? You there?'

'I'm here.'

'Quickly, tell me how my – '

'All things considered, they're fine. Adelina has moved in with her brother. After the funeral, she received quite a few letters from, well, she felt safer moving. We miss you, Joe.'

'I miss you – hello? *Pronto*?'

The line is dead.

Taking advantage of the operator, he asks to be connected to the *Milan Gazette*. Easily done. He reaches Alvise and fills him in briefly on what Vachris said about the men on the list and how there's no sign of Venturini.

'I'd like to speak with la Signora Greco.'

'Already set up,' says the journalist.

'Where shall I meet you?'

'I'm a bit pressed for time, so you're on your own. She expects you at her home.'

He thinks about all the house calls he's made over the years to the homes of wives: welcomed in by hopeful spouses, then shown the door by grieving widows.

'What's her address?'

Nine

I n a poor neighbourhood along the Navigli towards the docks, he rings the bell to a ground floor apartment. A little girl opens the door. She looks up at him. Not afraid so much as curious about the heavyset man in an overcoat and strange hat.

'*Ciao piccola*,' he says.

'Aurora,' says la Signora Greco, coming down the hall, wearing an apron, an oven glove on her hand, 'what have I told you?'

Putting her finger in her mouth, the child lowers her head but keeps an eye on the stranger.

'*Prego* Signor Velletri, please come inside.'

'*Permesso*,' he says, wiping his feet on the doormat and removing his derby.

'Here, let me take that, and your coat.'

The small kitchen smells of freshly baked bread. In a cot lies a baby boy, holding in his little hand a small wooden horse which he sucks on intently.

'This is Giona,' she says, 'and you've already met Aurora.'

He sits on the bench at a booth table in the corner. The girl, not taking her eyes from him, climbs up and kneels on the bench opposite. Set before her is a scrap of paper and some crayons. She takes a black crayon and holds it upright in her tiny fist.

'I'm busy baking,' says the girl's mother.

'It smells good.'

'Can I offer you anything? Coffee perhaps? I've just made some.'

'Please,' he says.

She removes the oven glove and goes to the stove.

'How do you take it?'

'*Lungo*,' he says.

Aurora smiles at his reply and draws a big, slightly lop-sided ball.

La Signora Greco brings two cups to the table and a plate of *biscottini*. Aurora is quick to grab one.

'Aurora, *educazione*,' says her mother, at which the little girl reaches over and offers him the biscuit.

He accepts. '*Gentilissima, grazie*,' he says, before popping the whole thing into his mouth, much to the child's delight. She takes one for herself, copying the detective, giggling as she does so. Her mother smiles and wags her finger.

'Can we talk,' the detective says, looking at the children.

La Signora Greco turns to her daughter. 'Aurora, why don't you show Signor Velletri your bear?'

She shakes her head and draws a smaller misshapen ball on top of the larger one.

'I'd like to meet your bear,' he says, smiling.

The girl considers him briefly before looking again at her drawing and then, setting down the crayon, bounds down from her seat and out the kitchen.

'*Vai piano, per piacere*,' says her mother.

'She's a character,' he says.

'And a handful,' she says, her eyes glowing. 'What news do you have?'

He sips his coffee, then lowers the cup to the saucer. 'My connection in New York tells me that there is no record of your husband.'

'Which means he didn't leave,' she says quietly.

'Yes, or that he is on the ship.'

'No, as I told you, Signor Velletri, my husband would not have left without saying goodbye to me. To his children.'

The detective looks across at the baby boy shaking the wooden horse about.

'Signora – '

'*Per favore*, call me Marianne,' she says.

'Marianne,' he says, awkwardly, 'the other women, do you know if their husbands disappeared in similar circumstances? I mean, without a goodbye, without a trace?'

She shakes her head. 'No, there was nothing like that. Their husbands took their leave and said that they would arrange passage for their wives once they'd settled, that was the agreement.'

'So these women accompanied their husbands to the station and saw them off?'

'The men were taken by automobile.'

'You mean they were picked up?'

'Yes, by the same that came for my husband the night he disappeared.'

'And you're sure of that? The same automobile?'

'It was an American model. One of those T Fords. Bright red and brand new. Hard not to remember. Besides, when you see one in this neighbourhood, you notice.'

Aurora's little footsteps come running down the hall. In her arms she holds a small bear. It's grey and fluffy. Its nose is missing and there are a few loose strands of thread in its place. The child holds the bear out to him, but she does not let him take it.

'What's his name?' he asks.

'Koala,' says the little girl, her bright eyes widening.

'But he isn't one.'

'Yes, he is,' snaps Aurora, pulling the bear into her arms.

'I'm sorry,' he says. 'You're right. I'm mistaken.'

She climbs back up to her place at the table. Her mother smiles. 'She's obsessed with Koalas, who knows why.'

Aurora sets the bear beside her and, picking up her crayon, continues to draw, colouring in the large circle with black.

'Can you tell me how your husband met his proposed employers?' says the detective.

'Is papa coming home?' says Aurora, her expression turning serious.

'*Presto tesoro,* go on with your picture,' says her mother, getting up from the table. She fetches her handbag and goes through the contents of her purse. 'Here,' she says, handing him a small card. 'He was given this number. I've tried calling it, but there is no response. It's been disconnected.'

On the card appears a phone number and the company name: Trades Associated.

'May I keep this?'

'Of course.'

Suddenly the baby lets the horse clatter to the floor, and he begins to wail, kicking his little legs.

Marianne bends down to retrieve the toy. 'He's hungry.'

The detective stands up. 'I'll let you get on with things.'

'*Grazie*, Signor Velletri,' she says. 'Aurora, let's say goodbye.'

The little girl shakes her head, keeping her eyes fixed on her drawing, where a small hat now appears on top of the small misshapen ball.

Outside, he takes the calling card from his pocket. Trades Associated. On the back in small lettering, he finds the name and address of the print shop. He decides to pay them a visit. But first he needs a change of clothes.

Ten

essed in workman's attire and a baggy flat cap, he strides downtown to Milan's commercial centre. The address on the calling card is Via della Moscova 34. On reaching the street, the print shop is easy to find. Parked outside a shop with a large window is a red Model T Ford Touring. A group of young men smoking cigarettes hang about the automobile. Well-dressed with slicked-back hair, greasy types. To the trained eye these *mafiosi* minions stick out like babes on a whisky barrel. He's come to the right place.

He lowers his cap and crosses the street. Seeing him approach, the young men cease their jabbering and drag on their cigarettes, their cheeks sinking in, then puffing out, exhaling curls of smoke. A few of the lippy fellas make comments about his size, calling him *nano ciccione*, but when he doesn't slow down, pumping his arms as he walks, they're quick to make way, sending their jeers after him as he enters the shop. Fine way to do business. Unless you don't need it.

Inside, a skinny man wearing wire rimmed glasses sits behind a desk checking over a ledger. At a glance, the man, with his pensive brow, has the appearance of a typical office clerk. Square and legit. But his deep frown lines and black hair streaked with white make him look like a young man who has aged prematurely. The detective knows the type, guys whose businesses have been taken over by threat and muscle. He almost feels sorry for him.

The clerk is so focussed on the books that he doesn't even look up. Another sign that actual customers are a thing of the past. Behind the clerk, he counts two printing presses. To the left, a door to a back office is closed. The top half of the back wall is fitted with a large mirror.

On the edge of the desk lies a stack of pamphlets bearing the familiar emblems of the Black Hand. He discreetly slips one into his back pocket, then raps his knuckles on the edge of the desk. The startled clerk looks up, the frown lines deepening before setting into what appears to be the poor fellow's natural expression of bewilderment.

'*Sì?*' says the man, shutting the ledger and shooting up to his feet.

'This is a print shop, right?'

The man adjusts his glasses, peers down at the ledger, then looks up again, focusing his eyes on the detective's chin, as if he's just found something there of interest. 'That's correct.'

'I'm an artisan, new to the city, perhaps you can help me.'

The man stares blankly at him, again fiddling with his glasses.

'I'm looking to advertise my business.'

'Oh, I understand,' he says, glancing behind him. 'But I don't think we – '

The door to the back office opens and a man marches out. 'One moment, Farini,' he says. Along with a distinct accent, he has a somewhat foreign appearance. Dressed in black, tight-fitting cavalry trousers tapering to leather boots and a waist length coat, buttoned left to right, it's as though the man has recently returned from the battlefield. His complexion is dark like a Moor and his close beard and moustache are meticulously fashioned. The banter of the young toughs outside stops suddenly, and the detective glances back to see them scampering off.

'Signor Ruiz,' says the clerk, 'I was just saying we don't – '

The man in black raises his hand, and the clerk shuts up and drops down in his chair, as if he were trained to do so.

'So you're a tradesman? What do you do exactly?'

'Carpentry,' says the detective, trying to place the man's accent. 'Shelving, furniture. Actually, looking at your office here, you could use some shelving, no?'

'Perhaps.' The man smiles, baring beautiful front white teeth. 'What is it we can do for you?'

'Ah, right, I was thinking I could have some ads printed, you know, to tack up around town.'

The clerk looks up at his boss, only to avert his eyes as he is shot a warning glance.

'Why don't you leave us the details.'

'The details?'

'Of what you'd like printed.'

'I could do that, yes, let me give it some thought.'

'You're not sure?' The man runs a hand down the side of his coat, as if irritated by a sudden itch.

'I just wanted to get an idea of prices before I commit.'

The clerk makes the mistake of reaching for the pile of pamphlets at the end of the desk. The man in black is quick to brush him aside and grab them. 'Well,' he says, slipping the pamphlets into the front of the ledger, 'that depends on the choices you make.'

'Choices?'

He tucks the ledger under his arm. 'The paper, typeface, how many words. Of course, it takes time, you see, we must set everything first, you get the picture.'

'I do,' says the detective. 'Let me get back to you…Signor Ruiz, was it?'

The man again glares at the clerk. '*Sì*, and you are?'

'Gugliemo Saulino.'

'Will there be anything else, Signor Saulino?'

'No,' he says, touching the peak of his cap. 'By the way, that's some machine you've got.'

'I'm sorry?' says Ruiz.

'The automobile out front, a Model T, isn't it?'

Ruiz twists his moustache, and his smile widens, revealing two yellowish canines. 'It belongs to one of our investors, isn't that so, Farini?' he says, gripping the clerk's shoulder.

The poor man adjusts his glasses and nods.

'There you go,' says Ruiz.

Just then, a second man wearing a costly pinstriped suit leaves the office. The detective recognises him instantly and knows that, given the chance, the man will recognise him, too. Fortunately, lighting a short, fat cigar and attending to one of the presses, the man takes little notice of him.

'You'll be hearing from me, signori,' says the detective.

Going out the door, he glances back to see Ruiz marching to the back of the room with the ledger, ignoring the man with the cigar who averts his eyes. The clerk hasn't budged but simply stares down at his empty desk.

Eleven

Back in Chinatown, the detective enters Finn's bar. He slaps down his baggy cap on the counter and orders a glass of chianti.

'Velletri,' says Finn, pouring the wine, 'don't take this the wrong way, but you're dressed like a goddam paperboy. A man of your experience. You need to move with the times. After all, it's 1909. A new decade is upon us.'

'Well, Finn,' he says, reaching for his glass. 'I like to think the times move with me.' He sips the chianti and drums his stubby fingers on the bar. 'Has there been any more trouble?'

'Not the type of trouble you mean, but business is quieter. People are nervous.'

The detective nods and glances at the sports page of the *Herald* spread out in front of Finn. The New York Giants lost to the Pittsburgh Pirates, denting their hopes of winning the National League. How he misses the game, and the New Yorkers' zany fervour for it.

'Can I use your phone?'

'Sure, go ahead.'

Finn sets the phone in front of him and takes some empty bottles out back. He gulps down the wine and dials. He's put through to the journalist's desk.

'How'd it go with la Signora Greco?' Alvise asks.

'She has tremendous faith in her husband, and that we'll find him.'

'It doesn't look good, though, does it?'

He takes the pamphlet from his pocket. 'No,' he says, 'but I have a lead. I need you to set up a meeting with the chief inspector?'

'You want to cuddle up with your ol' pal and have me play chaperone, is that it?'

'I'll explain when we meet, some place discrete.'

'How about my office?'

'That'll do. And tell Cattaneo to come alone.'

The detective walks back through the Chinese quarter. While most of the store owners know him, everybody seems on high alert, and the usual convivial chatter seems now to be conducted in whispers.

As he approaches the *pensione*, men disguised as chimney sweeps and labourers peer down at him from rooftops. Entering the courtyard, he's surrounded by armed guards. They chat wildly amongst themselves, as if they are arguing over who gets to keep what after they do away with him.

Xuan rushes out and utters a single syllable at which the men retreat behind the old fig trees.

'What's all this about?' he asks.

'Come with me,' she says.

Inside, the lobby shutters are closed. In the near darkness, he makes out the figure of Yang and the other maids, waiting, ready to attend to their mistress. He expects Xuan to lead him to her office, instead she walks into her rooms. He hesitates, but she turns and gives him a reassuring glance. From head to toe.

After leaving his shoes at the door, he enters after her. The room could not be more different from what he imagined. Hearing the Chinese opera music each evening has filled his imagination with scenes decorated with miniaturist paintings, oriental rugs, a tiger in a cage. Instead, the room is simple and modestly furnished. In the centre lies a low table with two single elongated cushions on either side. In the corner, beside a chaise longue, a gramophone and a stack of records sits neatly on a commode. In front of the shuttered window, hanging baskets of ferns unfurl above an extended inner windowsill filled with a variety of *penzai* in ceramic pots and vases of red anthurium and orchids. It pleases him to see that at least one element of his fantasy is true.

Xuan crosses her arms and sighs. 'Please Joe, you're not a schoolboy.'

He realises that he's still wearing his cap and slips it off.

'Better. Now sit, I've prepared some tea.'

He lowers himself awkwardly onto one of the cushions and crosses his legs, grateful that he's able to hide his threadbare socks beneath the table.

Xuan sets a tray with an earthenware teapot and two small bowl-like cups down on the table. She kneels opposite him and pours the tea. He takes up one of the cups. The scent of mint and jasmine is pleasant. The tea, Xuan's company, the room itself, makes him feel warm and calm. Something he has not felt in a long time. He savours the moment and again takes in his surroundings. On the commode, beside the gramophone, he now notices her long jade cigarette holder and a packet of French cigarettes, the strong, filterless brand favoured by infantrymen.

She follows his eyes and appears to read his thoughts.

'It's something I do in moments of leisure,' she says. 'Lately, there have been few of those.'

He nods. 'Doesn't it affect your voice?'

She covers her lips with her fingertips.

'I didn't mean to embarrass you. Your voice is beautiful.'

'You like opera, then?'

'I do, very much,' he says. 'Verdi and Rossini most of all, but yours, those arias you sing, well, I've never heard such music. Of course, the words are lost on me. But not their meaning, if that makes sense. The sadness, that I understand. You're obviously a trained singer. Was that before – '

Raising her hand, she stops him. Then she lifts her cup to her lips and sips the tea and sets it down again. 'You and I have a lot in common,' she says.

He isn't sure what she means, but he nods, wanting it to be true. He'd looked like a schoolboy, and now he feels like one. She gathers her loose hair, separates it in three, and begins to weave it into a single plait.

'We've both come from far away,' she continues, 'both of us with a past we prefer not to share, both of us are perhaps not what we seem, would you agree?'

He lowers his eyes. Never has he felt so disarmed in front of another person.

'But what if we were to share ourselves?'

He gulps more tea, gathers himself. 'I suppose it would be dangerous. I mean, there is a reason why, isn't there?'

'Would we be able to trust each other?'

He looks at her, trying to look past the mystery in which he himself has placed her. *Trust* He lets the idea rest in his mind, until he realises that he doesn't believe in it. How can he when he no longer trusts himself? He looks down at the empty cup in his hands.

'Would you like some more,' she asks, tying the end of the plait with a dark red ribbon.

He shakes his head and sets the cup down. 'I'd like to know what you plan to do.'

'Hao,' she says, staring towards the shuttered windows.

'What about him?'

'He's missing,' she says.

He inadvertently reaches for his foot, covering the thread-bare patch around his heel. He knows that in the times they live, the word *missing* often means *lost*, with its sense of permanency. *Gone.* 'I see,' he says.

'Hao is my general. And my closest friend. My people are looking for him. Good men are being killed.'

'You do realise who you're up against?'

'The same men you are.' She fixes her dark eyes on him.

He looks away. 'What are you asking me?'

'Can I trust you, Joe? Can we trust each other?'

He pushes his cup forward, lifts his head, holds her gaze, as much as he can bear to. 'I suppose we need to try,' he says.

Back in his room, he studies the pamphlet he'd taken from the print shop. The announcement of a meeting of the Black Hand. More propaganda to fuel the anarchists' cause. He thinks about the riots in Barcelona. The violent deaths of civilians caught up in the conflict. Social tension is high across Europe, creating the perfect working conditions for the criminal underground. As in New York, the Mafia are using the politicised Black Hand as a front to further their own illegal operations. He scans the pictures tacked on the back of his door. From amongst the mug shots of the Morello crime family, he takes down the picture of the man in the pinstriped suit he'd seen earlier. Giovanni Di Primo. The last time they'd met was at the Barrel Murder trial in which Di Primo agreed to testify against Morello and others in return for his freedom. A few months after Di Primo's release from Sing Sing, the body of Tommaso 'the Ox' Petto, Morello's most ruthless button man, was found in the woods. Both the police and the Mafia knew who was responsible. Yet here he is, in Milan, alive and apparently back in business. Obviously, Di Primo's expertise as a counterfeiter makes his life worth more than the loyalty and life of *il Bove*.

What concerns him is how this Ruiz fits in. The first impression was bad. The man could talk shop, but he wasn't buying any of it. He knows a killer when he sees one. The clerk clearly feared him, as did the young hoods out front. Then there is the question of the Model T Ford. They don't come cheap. Especially not when shipped over from the States. He suspects it belongs to Di Primo. While the smart bosses are wisely discrete in their operations, there are always one or two hapless Sicilian *capi* out of small, backward towns who can't help flashing around their ill-gotten *denaro*. One would think Di Primo had been in the game long enough to know better.

There is a knock at his door.

'Message from your friend,' Chupeng says. 'Three o'clock, Via Garibaldi, second floor.'

The detective nods and searches his pocket for some change. But the boy shakes his head and is gone.

Twelve

The newspaper office on Via Garibaldi is crammed. A low-pitched hum of activity rises from the newshounds grouped around a desk, all talking at the same time in hushed yet heated voices. There is the occasional loud command from the editor followed by renewed activity around a different desk, centred on a different item of news.

Outside Alvise's small office on the second floor, Gilberto Scalisi sits perusing a document held up close to his face. The detective doffs his hat, and the official from Rome nods, squinting with his close-set eyes.

Opening the office door, the detective finds the chief and Alvise waiting for him. With the large desk, covered with photographs, and a shelf overflowing with books, journals, and files, there is barely space for the three of them. There appears to be some logical order to things, but only Alvise himself can be sure. To the left there is another door with a sign that reads: **camera oscura / non entrare**

'Good of you to join us,' barks Cattaneo. 'What's this all about?'

'Sorry, let me get these out of the way,' says Alvise, gathering up the photographs: a collage of socialites, criminals, and corpses. He'd bet that many of the individuals in the first two groups ended up in the last.

'Alvise and I have been looking into something,' says the detective.

'Inchiostro is always snooping where he doesn't belong and if you're involved, I'm guessing it isn't just his neighbours' trash. Can you be a little more specific?'

'Give the man a chance,' says Alvise.

The inspector glares at the journalist who raises an apologetic hand.

'Go on,' says Cattaneo, 'but be quick.'

'A number of women have come forward claiming that their husbands have gone missing,' begins the detective.

'Nothing out of the ordinary there.'

'Right, only we did some checking on the men in question and four out of the five left Genoa with clean records and genuine prospects, only to pop up in New York involved in criminal activity connected with the Morello gang and their bogus affiliations with the Black Hand.'

'Why bogus?' says Alvise. 'The Black Hand are a serious political group.'

'Correct,' says the detective, 'but in New York the fear factor associated with the group, those symbols you've seen scrawled on the walls of Chinatown, are exploited by extortionist gangs who have little interest in politics.'

'The Mafia in other words?' says Cattaneo. '*Sentitemi,* I've got a city librarian busy deciphering Mandarin curses off a dead man's chest and my night patrols getting caught in cross-fire all down Via Alessandro Volta, so *santo cielo*, tell me why we're here, *per favore*.'

The detective clears his throat. 'We believe there is a connection between the killing of Gianni Gambino and these missing men.' From his pocket he takes the calling card given to him by Marianne and passes it to Cattaneo.

'Trades Associated?' says the chief. 'Never heard of it.'

'I think it's a front. We know these missing men were all without criminal records and with ambition to succeed in America. Easy pickings.'

'What's behind the front?'

'I went down to this address earlier, it's a print shop, and I'm guessing the base for a counterfeiting racket.'

'Hang on,' says Cattaneo, 'that's more than a leap of logic.'

The detective sets the pamphlet down on the desk. 'First of all, there's this. It's recruitment propaganda for the Black Hand. As I mentioned, in New York this group is linked with Morello.'

'That's this old friend of yours?'

'A friend of Don Vito,' says Alvise, folding his arms.

The inspector glares at the journalist.

'Don Vito Cascio Ferro,' says Alvise 'The boss running things in Sicily and up here in Milan. Organised crime.'

'I know who the Don is, Inchiostro,' says the chief, turning his scowl loose on the detective. 'So now you've got him on this crusade of yours, *complimenti*.'

'There's more,' says the detective.

'I don't doubt it.'

'While I was down at the print shop, I recognised a man named Giovanni Di Primo, a known counterfeiter. A couple of years back he killed a prominent member of the Morello gang in a vendetta.'

'Tommaso Petto?' says Alvise. 'Morello's button man?'

The detective nods. 'Otherwise known as *il Bove*, the Ox. Di Primo did some time in Sing Sing prison after taking a fall for Morello and his boys. Only they went on to double-cross him. The victim in the Barrel Murder case turned out to be a relative of his. Di Primo gave evidence in the trial that eventually saw Petto convicted.'

'This is some story,' says the inspector.

'It gets better. After a mix-up in the jail orchestrated by Morello's people inside the NYPD, Petto escaped and went into hiding. A few months later, after Di Primo's early release from Sing Sing, the Ox was found shot dead in his cabin in the woods.'

'Why was Di Primo released?'

'He made a deal with the public prosecutor. A considerably reduced sentence and eventual freedom in return for his testimony against Morello's gang.'

'Some good it did him,' says Alvise. 'Testifying against the Sicilian Mafia? He practically signed his own death sentence. How is Di Primo even still alive?'

'The man's a master counterfeiter. I'm guessing Don Vito is keeping him around. Until they find someone who can do what he does, he has a reprieve. But it's borrowed time.'

'And how does any of this solve my problems?' says the inspector.

'I don't have all the pieces yet, but my guess is that the counterfeiting operation is taking place at the print shop, which implicates Gambino, who I believe made the mistake of trying to push bad coin into the Chinese businesses as a way of laundering the money they're making through other means.'

'And so?'

'We need to raid the premises.'

'We?'

'I mean, you, Chief Inspector.'

Cattaneo shakes his head. 'The only evidence you have is some anarchist propaganda and a hunch about some *sfigato*, whom I've never heard of.'

'That's easily solved,' says Alvise, 'just wire New York. I'm sure they'll have files on Di Primo.'

'That's not going to happen,' barks the inspector. 'Don't you journalists follow the news?' He glances at the detective and then appears to choose his words carefully. 'Following a certain, recent incident in Palermo, the Americans are a little less forthcoming with information to Italian officials.'

The detective grimaces, reaching instinctively for the cigar in his pocket. Alvise studies him from the corner, then lowers his head pensively.

'*Senti*, you just have to take my word for it,' says the detective. 'The people Di Primo works for are bad news. But if you bust up this racket, you'll stop the fighting between the quarters. At least for now. And hopefully we'll find out what's happened to these missing men. You need to raid the print shop, and soon.'

'So you're in charge now?' says Cattaneo, standing up and adjusting his uniform. 'When do you propose we make our move?'

'Tonight.'

'Tonight?' The inspector reaches for his pocket watch.

'If they are operating on the premises, then it's likely to be afterhours.'

The chief scratches his head. 'OK, we'll look into it.'

'Don't take this too lightly, Chief Inspector. They may just be a bunch of fraudsters to you, but they're dangerous.'

'I get it,' says Cattaneo.

Out of the corner of his eye, the detective notices the shadow of the man from Rome pacing outside the door.

'I think somebody's getting impatient.'

Thirteen

D im light shines behind the drawn blinds of the print shop late into the night. Alvise and the detective wait in a café opposite. The descending mist obscures their view. There is no sign of the Model-T. Further down the street, Chief Inspector Cattaneo waits in his automobile with his right-hand man, Sergeant Lorenzo Bruno, and the young officer, Michele Esposito.

At 23:00, the police make their move, bursting into the unlocked door of the premises.

The detective watches, fidgeting with an empty coffee cup, his face just about pressed up against the café window.

'Let them handle it, Velletri,' says Alvise. 'The chief and his boys know what they're doing.'

'Maybe, but they don't understand who they're dealing with.'

'Wait for the all-clear, then we can go have a look.'

They don't need to wait long. Cattaneo comes out soon enough and waves them over. He doesn't look impressed. But when does he ever?

Inside, the room is lit by a few gas lamps around the heavy presses. A kid no older than 16 stands with his hands raised behind his head.

'Your suspicion was warranted,' says Cattaneo, grabbing a handful of newly printed pages. 'Have a look.'

Alvise and the detective both take a copy: an ad for a new hair lotion for men and anti-rash shaving cream.

'It's a crime,' says the inspector. 'The people responsible for these products deserve the maximum sentence.'

He tells Bruno and Esposito to wait outside. The men leave, the young officer giving the detective a sympathetic look.

'It's a good thing Scalisi isn't here,' Cattaneo continues. 'The last thing I need is word of this farce of a raid reaching my superiors in Rome.'

'I need to go home,' interrupts the kid.

'Button your trap and sit tight,' says the inspector.

'Have you checked the office?' says the detective, taking up one of the lamps. He sweeps past the kid and into the backroom. Apart from a two-way mirror and the fact that everything is suspiciously clean, there are no signs of anything incriminating. He opens one of the filing cabinets. Empty.

Cattaneo comes in behind him. 'Well, Sherlock?'

'This place has been cleaned. They knew we were coming.'

'*Senti*, I admit there may have been something going on, but that's true of half the offices in this city. Nobody is completely above board, but as for your counterfeiting spiel, there just isn't enough evidence.'

The detective marches out and grabs the kid by his shirt-front, roughing him up against the wall. 'How long have you been working here?'

'What are you doing?' says the inspector, following with the lamp. 'Let the boy go.'

'He knows something.'

'*Non so niente*,' says the kid, his eyes imploring the inspector to intervene. 'I'm just doing what I'm paid to do, *credimi*.'

'Since when?'

The kid lowers his eyes to the detective's scarred cheek. 'I don't know, a couple of weeks, maybe.'

'You're lying,' he says, threatening the kid with a fist.

'*Calmati*,' says Cattaneo, putting a cautious hand on the detective's shoulder.

'Wait,' says Alvise, kneeling beside one of the presses, 'bring the lamp over here.'

As the detective loosens his grip on the kid's shirt, the boy struggles free, stumbling to the floor, before finding his feet and running out.

'Let him go,' says the inspector, 'my men will hold him.'

Beneath the press lies a large rug. By the light of the lamp, a few sets of muddy footprints are visible, marking the floorboards from the entrance of the shop to the edge of the rug.

'The prints,' says Alvise, 'some of these are ours, but there are dry sets here.'

'It's been raining all day,' says Cattaneo, scowling.

'But the rug's clean.' He lifts the edge of it. Beneath lie more dry prints.

'Give me a hand,' says the detective. They shift the heavy machine off the rug, then, pulling it away from the floor, they find the outlines of a trapdoor, no more than a square metre.

They raise the door, and the detective lights the way down a wooden staircase to a basement room half the size of that above. Stale cigar smoke adds to the musty stench of rising damp. In the middle of the room stands a large table with two chairs on either end. An empty shelf against the far wall hides in the shadows.

'Looks like a meeting room,' says the inspector. On the floor, he finds a banknote. He holds it up to the light. The smudged figure of George Washington. A botched bill.

The detective pounds the table with his fist. '*Maledetti.*'

Tamanini arrives from forensics and they leave him to comb the room.

'I've had the kid taken down to the station,' says Cattaneo. 'Bruno will sweat him a little. In an interrogation, he makes you look like *Babbo Natale.*'

'They knew we were coming, Chief Inspector. How?'

'What about your little visit today?' says Cattaneo. 'You're not exactly subtle.'

The detective thinks back. 'No,' he says, 'someone played the rat.'

The inspector breathes heavily. 'Unlikely, I only briefed my guys in the ride over here.'

The detective paces in front of the clerk's empty desk. 'What about your man from Rome? Why isn't he here? I mean, if his job is to monitor your protocol.'

The inspector raises his eyebrows.

'He has a point,' says Alvise. 'The man seems rather shifty to me. And he was lurking outside my office earlier.'

'Scalisi? Come on, he's a deskman, he's more interested in writing notes – ' The inspector falls silent, brushing a hand back over his cropped hair.

'What?' says Alvise.

'He was asking questions.'

'And you gave him answers?' says the detective.

'Not all the details. Just enough to keep the man quiet.'

'Looks like he opened his mouth to someone.'

'Where was he this evening?' asks Alvise.

'He said he had to write a report.' The inspector shakes his head. 'No, I don't think he's involved in this.'

'There is one way to find out,' says the detective.

The inspector glowers, crossing his arms. 'I'm listening.'

Fourteen

T he detective sits in Parco Sempione, near the station.
The English tweed suit he borrowed irritates his skin.
The woollen coppola makes his scalp itch. He removes it,
scratches his head. He opens the *Milan Gazette*, but it's difficult to concentrate. It's ten o'clock. Alvise was due to call the
chief inspector at nine with a tipoff regarding a known courier
in the Chinese opiate trade and the location of an imminent
transaction. At the time of the call, the man from Rome
would be with the chief to discuss the day's course of action.
It's only a matter of time. That's if his plan works.

He looks around the park. An old woman breaks up bread
to feed the pigeons fluttering and pecking about her feet. One
of the birds lands on the bench beside him and he swipes at
it with his hand.

He reads the front page, dominated by local news of the
increased violence and vandalism on either side of Via Alessandro Volta. Residents are reluctant to cross the street at
night for fear of coming across another victim or becoming
one themselves.

As of this morning, there'd still been no sign of Hao. He
worries about Chupeng. The boy may be quick, but he has

the knack of finding himself in places he shouldn't be. He's just a kid, if that means anything anymore.

Two figures dressed in overcoats come through the park gates. He knows from experience that men who wear heavy coats in the summer are probably carrying guns, concealing *lupara*. The sawn-off shotgun is not a weapon one can hide in the seat of one's trousers. The men clock on him and sit on the bench beside the old woman. She gets up and moves off. She can obviously smell the stench of *mafioso*. They keep their eyes on him, as she totters away.

Time to execute the next part of the plan. First, he needs to make sure it's them. He folds his newspaper and walks to the park gate. Tossing the paper in the bin, he glances back to see the men rising from the bench. He crosses the street, enters a café and orders an espresso. Discreetly, he checks the rounds in his .38, then slips the gun back beneath his jacket. He sweetens the coffee with a sugar cube, drinks it, and leaves.

Outside, across the street, the men wait. Getting a closer look, the detective recognises the younger of the two men, who isn't really a man at all. Leaning against a lamppost Bonifacio Pipitone, the kid who worked for the recently deceased Pappalardo, smokes impatiently. Clearly, he hasn't given up his bad habits.

'*Bene ragazzi*, let's go for a walk,' the detective mutters to himself. He crosses the street and walks back through the gates of Parco Sempione. He glances over his shoulder to catch the older man slapping Bonifacio on the side of the head. They follow.

He exits the far end of the park, then ambles past the train station and along Via Luigi Canonica. A man with a camera coming towards him signals with a tilt of his flat cap as he passes. The men are still on his tail. Skirting the Chinese quarter, he picks up pace and enters the industrial zone. Outside a garage, a broad-shouldered man with a buzzcut attends to the engine of an automobile. Seeing the detective, he lowers the hood and precedes inside. The men are not far behind. He turns left down an alley. At the end, he sees the back door to a warehouse.

The door is unlocked, but in case the men have lost their way, he takes his time opening it.

Inside, the warehouse is lined on both sides with stacked crates. In the middle of the concrete floor is a chair. He wonders who has been so thoughtful. He takes a seat facing the door and waits.

The two men burst in, whipping their coats aside and raising their *lupara*. Their eyes flash about the room.

'Check the goods,' says the older man. Bonifacio moves quickly to the crates.

'How can I help you?' says the detective calmly, although his heart is racing. He has seen the mess a *lupara* makes.

The older man makes his way forward. 'Are you armed?'

'No,' the detective says, raising his hands, knowing that his hidden .38 is useless to him now.

'They're closed,' says Bonifacio.

'*Cazzarola*,' the older man curses, jabbing the shotgun into the detective's gut. 'What's inside?'

He was hoping to get them to say a little more but feeling the snout of the gun in his gut has weakened his resolve. It's time to say the word. He only wishes that they'd decided on something a little less auspicious.

'Something's wrong,' says the kid, squinting at the detective. 'I know you.'

The detective keeps his eyes on the older man.

'I know you,' repeats the kid, getting more agitated. 'Let's get out of here.'

'*Calmati, cazzo*. What's inside?' says the older man.

'Fireworks,' says the detective.

'*Che cosa?*'

There is no need to answer a second time. The door opens and the chief inspector enters with his Smith & Wesson revolver raised. From behind the crates, officers Bruno and Esposito spring out with their guns trained on the kid.

The older man turns his *lupara* on Cattaneo, but the inspector is quick to squeeze his trigger, shooting the man in the chest. Bonifacio with two guns pointed at his head wisely lowers his *lupara* and puts his hands up. The detective stands, reaching for his .38, then takes the gun from the kid who glares at him, still not making the connection. The detective isn't about to help him out.

Cattaneo kicks the shotgun away from the dead man and kneels beside him, checking for a pulse. 'He's dead.'

Alvise arrives on the scene. He adjusts his flat cap and quickly fixes a flash bulb to his camera. He seems excited to have the chance to shoot a living perp for a change. The kid is cuffed and escorted to the wagon. He chews his lips nervously. He may be young, but the police won't be able to get anything out of him. The detective knows the ways of *omertà* are instilled early on. And Bonifacio Pipitone is as tough and bull-headed as they come.

With hangdog eyes, Cattaneo watches as the corpse is carted away.

'You didn't have a choice,' says the detective. 'It's not like you shot him in the back.'

'At least it wasn't the kid,' he says, brushing off his mechanic's overalls.

'What about our man from Rome?' says the detective.

'Signor Scalisi is stewing in a cell as we speak. The moment I saw the men had taken the bait I made the call. We'll have Bruno ask him a few questions.'

'Sergeant Bruno is going to have his hands full. Maybe he could use some help,' says the detective, tossing aside the coppola, grateful to be rid of it. 'That kid's a tough Sicilian nut that won't crack. Believe me I've tried cracking a few before. The only thing they spill is blood.'

'You've got a poetic turn of phrase, I'll say that. But still, I'd prefer my suspects to be recognisable when it's time to appear in court.'

Alvise joins them, looking satisfied. 'Well, that worked like a charm.'

'You did well,' says the detective. 'You may have a future in law enforcement.'

The inspector raises his eyebrows. 'I'll leave you boys to pat each other on the back. I have a report to write and some bad apples to press. I'll keep Inchiostro in the loop if I get anything out of them.'

'Don't hold your breath,' says the detective.

'I'm optimistic. Our man from Rome may be a rat snitch, but he doesn't have the stomach for *pasta fredda* and a dark cell.'

Fifteen

After the inspector rounds up his squad and heads back across town, Alvise and the detective make their way towards the Chinese quarter.

'How'd you know that would work?' asks the journalist.

'Don Vito thrives on power, and the Chinese monopoly on the opium trade is a chunk of the enterprise he doesn't have control over.'

'Not yet,' says Alvise.

'Right, so if he thinks that he can sabotage their trade by taking their merchandise, then he'll jump at the chance.'

'The question is who did Scalisi call? I doubt he contacts the Don directly.'

'I'm hoping you'll be able to find that out. At the print shop yesterday, there was a man I didn't like the look of.'

'A capo?'

'Not sure. There's something different about him. Most capos come through the ranks with blood on their hands, but once they're promoted, they simply sit back to enjoy the *denaro*. This guy seemed more like a button man, hands-on and aggressive, but with some say on how the operation is run.'

'A button man with clout?'

'*Esattamente*. See if you can dig something up. He's certainly someone people will remember. There was a slight Spanish lilt in his accent, and the clerk made the mistake of using his name. Ruiz.'

'Could be fake? You know what these guys are like.'

'Maybe, but he seemed put out by it.'

As they reach the edge of Chinatown, Chupeng rushes up to meet them. His eyes are wide, and he tugs at the detective's arm.

'Come Signor Velletri. No time.' Then he turns and runs. The detective and Alvise follow, doing their best not to lose the fleet footed boy.

Not far from the market, a crowd of Chinese has gathered at a corner of an alley. At the sight of the two Italians, the Chinese step aside, some voices rise angrily. A woman tries to pull Chupeng towards her, but he brushes her aside and runs down the alley. They follow the boy. The crowd falls silent.

At the end of the alley, men stand solemnly around a wheelbarrow. Chupeng stops in his tracks, lowers his head, and waits.

'These are Xuan's men,' says the detective.

He and the journalist proceed with caution. The men recognise him as the lodger from the *pensione* but do not seem pleased. In the wheelbarrow lies a dead body. Naked, his arms and legs hanging out, Hao has been stabbed multiple times. Skull and crossbones carved across his chest. It's not how he'd like to remember this gentle man with his silent dignity.

Alvise reaches for his camera, but the detective grabs him by the wrist.

'Not here,' he says.

The journalist nods. They both lower their heads, then leave. There is no sign of Chupeng.

At the exit to the alley, the crowd grows increasingly vociferous. Wailing and shouting. Hearing the commotion, more people arrive. Soon there will be a mob. The detective remembers what a crowd rallied to action can do. Back home, the lynching of the gang of Sicilians known as the Matrangas' Gardeners in New Orleans set a precedent for future acts of mob justice. Something he doubts is unique to the other side of the Atlantic.

They continue walking briskly up Via Paolo Sarpi. Away from the crowd, Alvise stops and readies his camera.

'I wouldn't get too close,' says the detective. 'These people have just lost a respected member of their community. They're not going to appreciate the likes of you poking that camera in their faces.'

'The likes of me?'

'An Italian from the wrong side of the street.'

'I'll take my chances.'

'It's not safe for you here, Alvise.'

'I'm a journalist,' he scoffs. 'This is news.'

'Well, get your pictures, then see what you can find out about Ruiz.'

'What are you going to do?'

'I need to get back to the *pensione* in case things 'round here escalate. Call me the minute you find out anything. If you don't reach me, try again.'

'Shouldn't you be getting out instead?'

The detective looks down the street. The crowd quietens. All that can be heard is the clunking of the wheelbarrow as one of Xuan's men pushes the shrouded body through the assembled mourners.

He hurries towards the *pensione*. He needs to make sure that Xuan is safe. If the Mafia have taken out her right-hand man, then she'll be next. She is bound to retaliate. It is not a case of if but of when and how. Both of which could determine whether it's going to be safe for him to continue living where he is. The lodger of *la Madrina di* Chinatown.

Finn and Ofelia stand outside their bar, looking on as people begin to close their shops and take part in the procession. It seems peaceful enough. Many of the women and children are carrying flowers and wreaths.

'What the hell's happening, Velletri?' says Finn.

'There's been a murder. His name was Hao, he was – '

Ofelia reaches for her husband's hand. 'We knew him,' she says, her eyes downcast.

'He came to see us often.'

'For your tribute?'

'Yes, but not only,' says Finn. 'He was a true gentleman.'

He nods. '*Sentite*, things might get bad 'round here, you should take care.'

'Thanks, Joe,' says Ofelia. 'We've seen it get bad before.'

'Perhaps,' he says, looking at the outside wall with its fresh paint. 'I'll check in on you soon, be safe.'

Security along Via Paolo Lomazzo is tight. Despite knowing who he is, Xuan's men stop and search him before he reaches the courtyard. He is then escorted to the entrance.

Locking the door to her rooms, Xuan is dressed demurely in a long black dress, her hair tied up with a ribbon of white cotton. In the lobby, Yang and a few other maids, dressed similarly in simple black dresses, attend to a set of wreaths.

Xuan rushes towards him. 'Joe,' she says, composing herself. 'I was worried, that, well, you know.'

'Yes,' he says, squeezing her hand.

'I must visit Hao's family.'

'It isn't safe.'

She touches his face with the back of her hand. 'No, it isn't,' she says, smiling sadly. 'Would you like to come with me?'

Before he can reply, she turns to Yang and the maids and tells them to prepare to leave. The young women talk quietly amongst themselves and in pairs take up the wreaths and move ahead of Xuan into the courtyard. The doors to the *pensione* are locked and a couple of heavyset men with rifles slung over their shoulders remain on guard.

He walks beside Xuan. No words pass between them. Her eyes watch the road ahead. On reaching Via Paolo Sarpi, they join the procession of mourners. All around them are Chinese, stern faced and sombre. A few men who he knows to be Xuan's personal bodyguards walk behind and ahead of them. He clenches and unclenches his fists.

They are just turning a corner when from the rooftop a glint of sunlight catches his eye. Instinctively he grabs Xuan and pulls her into him, turning his body towards the closest wall. A knife rips through the arm of his tweed jacket. Within seconds they are closed in by men and women, whom he had assumed were ordinary Chinese citizens. Instead he sees now they stand, each of them, men and women, guns and knives drawn, their backs turned towards Xuan, surrounding their leader, ready, in search of the assailant. Xuan's personal guards dart through the streets in pursuit of a man in black with laced leather boots fleeing across the rooftops with feline agility.

Sixteen

Despite the attack on her life, Xuan proceeds to the home of Hao's family. His widow is unwell with grief, and the flowers are accepted by Hao's son, who with his prominent cheekbones, tall stature, and warm eyes, resembles his father.

The streets are crowded, and the mood is heavy with an edge that could easily be swayed towards violence. He is sure that should Xuan give the word, she'd have an army behind her. She speaks to Hao's son, and he nods and goes back inside.

She unties the ribbon from her hair. 'Give me your arm.'

He lowers a bloody hand from his torn jacket.

'Take it off.'

He removes the jacket gingerly. One of the maids is quick to take it from him.

'It's only a flesh wound,' he says.

'Perhaps,' Xuan says, tying the ribbon tightly around his arm.

Hao's son returns with a man's overcoat and a beret. Xuan puts on the coat, concealing her long hair beneath it. Then she puts on the beret.

'We can leave now,' she says.

He smiles. More evidence of his theory. Her beauty shines through no matter what she wears.

'Perhaps we should return another way,' he says, 'to avoid the crowds.'

She looks at him thoughtfully, as if seeing her reflection in his eyes. She turns to her maids, sends them ahead of her, then dismisses all but one of her guards.

'Come,' she says, 'follow me.'

Through a series of backstreets and secret passages, they reach the *pensione*, where security has been doubled. Men in black rush about like ants. He follows Xuan inside. She unlocks her rooms, where they are attended to by Yang, who, having listened carefully to all her mistress has told her, runs off again.

Xuan removes the overcoat and beret, discarding them on the headrest of the chaise longue. She places a wooden chair in the middle of the room.

'Let's have a look at you,' she says.

He glances at the chair, feeling a tinge of nervousness.

'Come now, Joe,' she says, taking him gently by the shoulders and pushing him forward. 'Sit.'

Two maids arrive carrying between them a wooden basin which they set down beside him. Steam rises from the water. Yang returns carrying some washcloths, a leather bag, and a neatly folded white shirt.

The door is closed, and they are left alone. Xuan fetches scissors from amongst the implements on her windowsill.

'What are you going to do with those?' he asks.

'Relax,' she says. 'You forget that I'm a practiced surgeon.'

'Yes, but I'm not one of your plants.'

'You're right, they're braver patients. They don't moan so much.'

She comes slowly towards him, pointing the sharp blades at his arm, then, rising the edge of the torn shirt, she cuts up the length of his sleeve, then across to his collar, so that the left side of his shirt falls away.

'You could have just asked me to take it off.'

'That's a good idea.'

He shakes his head and unbuttons his shirt, removing what's left of it.

The cut on his arm is deep. He hates to think of what harm the blade would have done had the tweed jacket not taken off some of the edge.

Xuan soaks one of the washcloths in the hot water and cleans the blood from the wound. He winces. She rinses the cloth in the water, his blood running into it like spilt red ink, and again she wipes away the fresh blood that streams down his arm.

'Hold this,' she says, pressing the cloth against the wound.

He does as he is told, and she ties it tightly with a leather strap.

'That should stem the bleeding.'

She stands and strides across to an ornate cabinet in the corner and returns with a bottle of cognac and two brandy glasses. She pours them each a generous dose. 'Here,' she says, 'for the pain.'

He drinks it down in one gulp and sets the glass aside. It's good stuff, and he feels his head clear, a sense of calm sweeping over him, like he's just slipped into a warm bath. She relaxes beside him, resting on the chaise longue. She reaches for the beret and adjusts it neatly on top of the overcoat.

'Don't blame yourself,' he says.

'Hao has been my friend for a long time. We've lived through a lot together. If it weren't for him, my life would be very different.'

'You knew him in China, then?'

'Hao worked for my family doing much of what he did for me here. He was an advisor to my father, and his bodyguard.'

'Where are your family now?'

She takes breath quietly. Her eyes seem to stare into him. 'Are you prepared to tell me your secrets too?'

He looks away. He feels a sudden, heightened awareness of his own skin, senses the ugly flaring up of his scars.

She reaches across, taking one of his hands in hers. 'My family are in Jingzhou,' she says quietly, 'in the district of Shashi, on the banks of the Yangtze River. They are wealthy, and powerful. They had plans for me, for my marriage. I did not share those plans, and so I escaped.'

'With Hao's help,' he says.

'He gave up everything for me. Including his family.'

'But his wife and son, I met –'

'He started a new life. A new family.'

He stares at the overcoat and the beret. 'Did he ever hear from his other family again? Didn't they try to find him? Haven't your family tried to find you?'

'That was not possible,' she says. 'My father had people looking for us, dangerous people. Hao knew that they'd be watching his family. He knew he risked their lives, that is, if they weren't dead already.'

'But why?'

'Why did he do this for me?'

'Yes.'

She averts her eyes and shakes her head. 'I don't know. It would have been an insult to ask,' she says. 'And he cared enough never to tell me.'

In the light of the lamp beside her, he notices for the first time the tiny splinter like scars beneath her left eye. Her hands, her long graceful fingers, are cool and soft. And he understands why Hao was prepared to sacrifice so much, and knowing for whom it was made, he comprehends why the decision was no choice at all.

Encouraged by the cognac, he turns her hand and traces the lines on her palm, comparing them to his own.

'Joe,' she says.

'I don't think I – '

She shifts to the edge of the chaise longue. 'There's no need,' she says. 'Not now at least. If I have told you something about my life, it's to thank you. For what you did today. *Xièxiè*.'

He tries to speak, but she shakes her head and gently pulls her hands free of his.

She rises and goes to the leather bag, opens it, and takes out a vial of clear liquid and some cotton gauze. 'Now, let's have another look at you.' She undoes the leather strap and removes the bloodstained cloth. 'The bleeding has stopped,' she says, dabbing the wound gently. 'Does it hurt?'

'I don't feel a thing,' he lies.

She applies some of the disinfectant, which burns, and then wraps it tightly up in the gauze, fastening it with a knot.

'Where did you learn that?'

'The knot?'

He nods.

'My father,' she says coldly. 'He had no sons.'

'Xuan,' he says, 'what will you do now?'

'About Hao's death?'

'How are you going to end all this?'

Quietly she seems to consider his question, packing the gauze and vial back into the leather bag. Everything she does is done with such grace that even the most mundane actions seem like a dance. Then she returns the scissors to the windowsill and stands facing her garden. 'If my plants do not see the light of day soon, they will die.'

That is her reply, and she picks up the white shirt that Yang left for him and begins to unbutton it, walking back towards him. He stands, feeling a little unsteady on his feet. She passes him the shirt, then helps him into it, so that he doesn't snag it on the dressing.

'We are going to help each other,' she says. 'The men who started this are the ones you are after. These counterfeiters.'

'How do you know what I've been up to?'

'You're forgetting that you are living under my roof, and where you go and who you see is known to me.'

'You spy on me?'

'Watch you, Joe. For your protection, and mine.'

'I understand what Gambino wanted. He isn't alone. The organisation he's with are expanding. They want Chinatown.'

'I won't allow that to happen. It would hurt the Chinese businesses.'

'But it wouldn't hurt you,' he says, tucking in his shirt. 'You could make a lot of money.'

'If you hurt the Chinese businesses, you hurt the Chinese quarter, you let the outsiders in. You hurt me and make me weak.'

'So, what's next?'

'You tell me.'

There is a knock at the door.

'Signor Velletri,' says Yang, 'there's a call for you.'

'Thank you,' he says. 'Maybe this is the answer.'

'Velletri,' says Alvise, 'I think we've got something. But we need to be quick. Meet me at Stazione Centrale.'

'Why?' he says, clutching his arm.

'My guy Martinelli with the F.S. says Giacomo Venturini has just booked a ticket. He'll be on the 18:30 train to Genoa.'

Seventeen

The dark grey clouds bunch around Stazione Centrale. Locomotives shunt into position, passengers say their goodbyes and board, whistles blow, and they depart. Dressed in F.S. uniforms, Alvise and the detective stand just outside the dining car. The detective feels the tightness of the conductor's jacket around his wound.

'I'm sorry there wasn't anything in your size,' says Alvise.

'It's not that,' he says.

Alvise takes a hip flask from his pocket. 'Try this. Grappa. Made it myself. It'll take the sting off.'

'From the smell of it, it'll take off more than that.' He takes a swig and shuts his eyes.

'That's it. Best medicine there is. You were lucky.'

'That's me, Lucky Velletri.'

'There's a name for you if you ever switch sides.'

'Do you think this plan is going to work?'

'After all the trouble Martinelli went to get these uniforms, let's hope so. The train guards will keep a low profile until we've done a full sweep of the cabins.'

'I'll take the front of the train and you start from the back. If you find our guy, you come get me.' The detective slips the photograph of Giacomo Venturini from his wallet. 'Here, take this.'

'You sure?'

'Unlike you, I have a photographic memory,' he says, winking. 'You didn't say anything to Marianne, did you?'

'I'd rather be sure,' says Alvise. 'I've a bad feeling about this.'

The detective groans and takes another swig and returns the flask to Alvise who takes a sip of his own.

'You sure you're up for this?'

'Let's go.'

They head in opposite directions. The detective moves to the front of the train. The calm he felt in the company of Xuan has worn off and he's left with the sting of his wound and the heady kick of the grappa. He takes a deep breath and opens the door to the first cabin. Inside, a man and a woman sit opposite each other in silence. He assumes that they are strangers to each other, but, collecting their passports for inspection, he sees that they are in fact husband and wife. French citizens. Monsieur and Madam Bulteau. The man regards him impatiently, while the woman, with an air of melancholy, gazes out the window. Thanking them, he returns their passports. Neither says a word, instead, they continue to stare past each other. '*Bon voyage*,' he says, closing the cabin door.

He makes further checks. One cabin after the other. Families, businessmen, soldiers on leave. In another cabin, a more seasoned traveller seems put out by the request and, instead, hands the detective his ticket.

'Passport only,' he says, adjusting his conductor's cap.

'What's the meaning of this?' says the man.

'Routine check.'

'I demand a better answer than that,' says the man, losing his temper.

The detective, trying to keep his own cool, shrugs.

'Signore, I could give you another answer, but then I may need to check your bags as well.'

The man shuts his mouth and produces his passport. The detective, savouring the moment, takes a little more time than is necessary looking over Signor Pietro Gori's documents. Small beads of sweat dot the man's brow as he loosens his tie. '*Grazie mille, Signore,*' he says eventually, returning the man's passport with all the politeness he can muster. '*Buon proseguimento.*'

The second to last cabin is full. Together with a family – husband and wife and their young son – there sits a man dressed in a white linen suit. While checking the couple's passports, he notices the man eyeing a trunk and briefcase in the rack above with increasing agitation.

He thanks the couple and smiles at the boy, who looks wide-eyed at the conductor's uniform, with its red stripes down the leg.

'Passport,' he says to the man, keeping his voice firm, despite the sudden race in his pulse.

'*Certo,*' says the man, '*un attimo.*'

With his linen suit and cocksure attitude, the man's Sicilian accent does little to dissuade the detective's suspicion. Attempting to play it cool, the Sicilian searches his side pockets, from which he takes out a pack of cigarettes and a pocketbook of matches before eventually producing his passport.

The picture in the passport is of a younger version of the man in the linen suit. There is a sudden icy sting in his wound.

'Giacomo Venturini?' he says, raising his eyebrows.

The couple glance across to their fellow traveller.

'*Eccomi qua,*' he says, reaching for his lapels with showman like bravado.

'Going far?' asks the detective, holding on to the passport, scrutinizing the quality of the forgery.

'Genoa,' says the man. 'What's it to you?'

'And is this all your luggage?'

The man straightens his back against the seat. 'That's my business,' he says, reaching out his hand.

The detective looks squarely at the imposter, making sure he's not mistaken and then returns the passport. The man glances at his own picture, then slips the document back into his pocket. He crosses his legs, left over right.

The detective doffs his cap to the couple and ruffles the boy's thick hair. 'You might consider a trip to the dining car,' he says to the family. 'I hear there's a special on *gelato*.'

He closes the cabin door and quickly makes his way back along the train in search of Alvise. He finds the journalist backing out of a cabin, fending off a little old lady who appears to have taken a liking to him.

'We've got him,' the detective says, grabbing Alvise by his shoulders.

'Venturini? You found him?'

'Not exactly,' he says. 'It's his name on the passport, but not his picture. And there's another man in possession of it.'

'What's happened to the real Venturini?'

'First things first,' says the detective. 'We need to get off this train and we're taking this imposter with us.'

'There's a stop at Novara, in about ten minutes.'

'Then we need to move fast.'

'So we go in and nab him. There are two of us.'

'Don't forget my *amico* here,' he says, opening his jacket to reveal the .38. 'Problem is he shares the cabin with a family. I tried to get them to the dining car, but I don't know if they took the hint. We need to get him out of there without getting him too riled. He's bound to be packing something.'

'Let me try,' says Alvise. 'He already knows you, so how about I tell him that he's been upgraded to first class, compliments of the conductor?'

'It's worth a try. Let's go, quickly.'

Entering the dining car, he can't believe their luck. Sitting at the bar, the briefcase on the stool beside him, the Sicilian is busy arguing with the waiter.

'I was told there was a special on *gelato*,' he says, 'and now you're saying there ain't none, *che cazzo*.'

'Here,' the detective says quietly, passing Alvise his gun. 'Man the door on the far end. Don't let anyone in, or him out.'

The Sicilian looks up, recognising the conductor's uniform. '*Eccolo là*.' He points the detective out to the perplexed waiter.

With his hands raised apologetically, the detective strides up to the man. 'Signor Venturini, *giusto*?' he says.

The Sicilian nods, holding on to the briefcase. 'He's telling me there's no *gelato*.'

The detective stands beside him, putting his hand on the Sicilian's back. 'How can that be?' he says. Then, grabbing the man forcefully by the neck, he slams his head down onto the bar. 'Move,' he shouts to the waiter. 'Watch that door. Nobody gets in, *capito*?'

The waiter does as he is told. The Sicilian tries to reach into his pocket, but the detective, still holding the man's head against the bar, grabs him now by the wrist and twists his arm behind his back.

'*Chi cazzo sei*?' says the Sicilian, gritting his teeth.

'We're cutting your trip short,' says the detective. 'Alvise, get the gentleman's briefcase.'

Alvise leaves his post and picks up the briefcase.

'*Che cazzo fai*?' The Sicilian struggles, kicking out at the bar, trying to push himself back, hoping they'll fall. The detective obliges, yanking him back, pulling him from the barstool.

'Alvise, show him we're not fooling around.'

The journalist points the .38 at the Sicilian, who, down on his knees, still does his best to free himself. Seeing the gun, he holds still. The detective grabs his other arm and hoists him to his feet.

The train begins to slow. Signs for Novara flash by.

'This is us. Now let's go, nice and slowly.'

'What about my trunk,' says the Sicilian.

'I'm sure it will be waiting for you in Genoa. Perhaps you'll visit one day.'

The next train to Milan is not for another hour. The detective doesn't fancy hanging about at a train station with the stubborn Sicilian who remains fidgety, his eyes shifty, just waiting for a chance to make a run for it. The detective doubts Alvise has it in him to shoot a running man.

'We have to get out of here without making a scene,' he says. He grips the Sicilian by the neck. 'If you feel the urge to scream, I'll pop you in the mouth.'

'*Vaffanculo,*' says the man. The detective knocks him on the nose with his fist. The Sicilian groans through clenched teeth.

'I warned you. I don't like you and the way things are going I'm going to like you a lot less by the time we're done.'

Avoiding the city centre, they make their way around the back of the station, where they sneak through a fence into a trainyard. They find an old brick building that's barely standing, its walls toppled, the roof caved in after a fire.

'You're breaking my arm,' says the Sicilian, as they step through the debris inside. 'You don't know who you're messin' with.'

The detective tightens his hold on the man's arm. 'Take off your tie, Alvise.'

The journalist slips the gun in the seat of his trousers and removes his tie.

'Bind his hands good and tight.'

The detective holds the man's wrists together, asserting enough pressure to keep him from trying anything.

'The less you struggle, the less painful this is going to be,' says Alvise. He winds his tie around the man's wrists and then secures it with a good scout's double knot. 'That should hold you.'

They sit the Sicilian on the ground in the corner. The detective removes the passport from the man's pocket.

'Where's Giacomo Venturini?' he asks.

'You're looking at him,' says the Sicilian, grinning. The detective smiles back, then punches him full in the mouth.

'*Cazzo*,' says the Sicilian, spitting blood.

'That's just me asking nicely,' says the detective. 'Try again. Where's Venturini?'

The man shakes his head and spits more blood.

Alvise opens the briefcase. Beneath a clean shirt and a girlie mag, he finds a pocketbook with documents belonging to Giacomo Venturini: birth certificate, diplomas. They all appear to be originals. There'd be no need to forge them. The entire bottom of the case is lined with banknotes. They are not new and to the unsuspecting eye, they look legit.

The detective grabs the Sicilian by his shirt front. 'Saving up for something?'

'It's not my money,' says the man.

'Whose then?'

The Sicilian's cocksure smirk returns. 'You don't want to know,' he says.

He grips the Sicilian's throat. 'I'm guessing whoever it is won't be happy that you've gotten yourself snatched and lost their money.'

The Sicilian gasps for air, his eyes on the contents of the case. 'You're better off letting me go,' he wheezes. 'We can make a deal.'

'A deal? No need, we'll get what we want from you.' He shoves the man back, knocking his head against the brick wall. 'Alvise, you sit tight, I'm going to make a call. You've got the gun. He tries to run, you shoot him.'

The Sicilian winks, trying to unnerve the journalist. The detective walks up and kicks the man in the ribs causing him to keel over. 'That's a reminder of what you're in for.'

The detective runs from the trainyard, towards the city centre. He enters the first café he finds and makes a call, giving their precise location. He races back to the trainyard.

The Sicilian lies quietly, curled in on himself. His face bloodied. Alvise shrugs. 'He was making too much noise.'

'Let's just hope he can still make the noises we want to hear,' says the detective, putting out his hand and taking back his gun.

In less than an hour, Xuan herself, wearing red leather driving gloves, arrives in a fancy, yellow and black Lion-Peugeot. They force the Sicilian onto the floorboard behind the seat. While the detective sits up front with Xuan, Alvise gets in the back, his shoes on the Sicilian, keeping him docile. The fight has gone out of him. He's stopped talking. Not a good sign. A silent Sicilian is no use to them.

Back in Milan, Xuan drives them to a warehouse well hidden in the backstreets of the Chinese quarter. Even Alvise is impressed.

Two workmen open the large doors. With the vehicle inside, they shut them again. Xuan, removing her red gloves, gives orders, and the same two men hurl the Sicilian from the Peugeot and drag him into a backroom.

'You've had a long day, Joe,' says Xuan, 'We all have. Let's get some rest.'

'What about him?' he asks.

Another man leaves the room carrying Alvise's tie. He is tall and wears a black tunic over wide, cotton trousers. His hair is long and dead straight with a fringe that hides his eyes. With his broad, pink lips and high cheekbones, his features are almost feminine. He extends a strong, bony hand covered with tattoos that run up his wrist and disappear beneath his open sleeve. The journalist warily takes his tie and bundles it into his pocket.

'He'll have the night to reflect,' Xuan says. 'I'm sure he'll have something to tell us in the morning.'

They all watch as the silent man seems to float back to the room. The door shuts behind him.

They exit the warehouse from a side door. As they walk out into the misty night, guided by Xuan through a warren of alleys, the Sicilian's screams ring out. The man has found his tongue.

Back in his room at the *pensione*, the detective slides the Sicilian's briefcase under his bed for safekeeping. He gets undressed, carefully taking off the tight-fitting jacket. It had felt good to be in uniform again. Removing his shirt, he sees that the dressing around his wound is still in place. There is a small pink stain. He thinks that perhaps he should clean the wound, but he is too exhausted. He lies on the bed and shuts his eyes. And yet, he still sees the delicate spray of splinter-like scars, a wave of jet-black hair.

Eighteen

'Joe, it's time to wake up.' He opens his eyes to the pale light of another grey morning. Xuan stands by the window, securing the shutters before tying back the curtains.

'Did you sleep well?' She walks to the door and opens it. Yang enters with a basin of hot water. He sees the familiar leather medicine bag already on the dressing table.

'How long have you been here?' he says, scrambling for his trousers.

'Long enough to know you snore like a bear.' She smiles and nods to Yang who gathers the uniform up from the floor and leaves.

'Come,' she says, 'let's get you cleaned up.'

'There's no need,' he says, 'I mean, I can manage.'

'This isn't about what you can do.'

He sits at the dressing table. She unwraps the gauze and once again performs the ritual of cleansing his wound with hot water. He watches her in the mirror, noticing her interest in the scars on his body.

'Do you want to ask me about them?'

She shakes her head. 'They're not that mysterious,' she says. 'I can see what they are. And as to what you've done to deserve them, well, that was made clear to me.'

In the mirror, her eyes meet his own, and he feels himself about to smile, but then she douses his wound in the clear liquid, which, without the courage of cognac, burns like fire. He grimaces, and she wraps his wound in fresh gauze.

'Thank you, Xuan,' he says.

She stands behind him, her hands on his bare shoulders, staring into the mirror. And for a moment they stay just like that, saying nothing. *Una natura morta.* A still life.

Striding ahead up Via Canonica, Chupeng shows him the way back to the warehouse. In his role as messenger and guide, the boy has become more serious. There is a look of quiet determination in his eyes. At that age, he was shining shoes outside the police headquarters on Mulberry Street, drinking up the stories told by some of the toughest Irish cops working the Lower East Side. Everybody has to start somewhere, but he wonders where the boy's career path will lead. No doubt Hao's death has affected him. He recalls the ghastly images of the two constables, the black and the white guards, the spirit guides to the underworld. It saddens him to think of the quiet Chinese gentleman being accompanied to the afterlife by the likes of them.

In the light of day, with the bustle of the market, the come-and-go of delivery lorries, and the hustle of hawkers, the streets surrounding the textile and leather workshops lack the illicit edge of the night before. But on entering the warehouse, the grinding saws of the workers bring back the memory of the Sicilian's screams.

There is no sign of the tall, tattooed man or either of the workmen. The door to the backroom is open. Inside, the windowless room is lit by a gas lamp hung from an iron hook. He expects to find the man bloody, but the only signs of physical harm come from the cut lip and bruised torso that he and Alvise had themselves inflicted.

He pulls up a chair in front of the Sicilian, but before he has asked a single question, he can tell by the pure dread in the once cocky man's eyes that the canary is ready to sing.

He arrives at the newspaper around ten carrying the Sicilian's briefcase. He called ahead and arranged once again to meet Chief Inspector Cattaneo at Alvise's office. He relayed the message that the news was good, so he is surprised to find the inspector wearing one of his deep scowls.

'What's happened?' asks the detective, shutting the door behind him.

'It's the man from Rome,' says Alvise.

Cattaneo nods. 'They got to him. He was found in his cell this morning. Suffocated in his bed.'

'Well,' he says, hanging up his coat and derby, 'at least you know who killed him.'

Alvise and the inspector look at each other.

'He was alone in the cell,' says Cattaneo.

'I guess your rat problem is bigger than you thought.'

The chief shoots the detective a cold look.

'Did you get anything from him, before – '

'Nothing,' says the inspector. 'He pleaded his innocence till the end, saying that he'd been sent by Rome, as though he'd had the sanctity of the Pope.'

'I wouldn't be surprised if this went up that far,' Alvise says.

'Enough of that,' says Cattaneo. 'Tell us why we're here.'

'Our man talked,' says the detective.

'Which man?' says the inspector, pulling a hand down his haggard face.

'You didn't tell him?' the detective asks Alvise who shakes his head and raises his hands in defence.

'Tell me now, *santo cielo.*'

'We caught one of the Morello gang on his way to Genoa.'

'Caught how?'

'Never mind that for now,' says the detective.

The chief bites his lip and gestures for him to continue.

'He was booked on the ship heading for New York this evening. His real name is Antonio Caruso, a Sicilian. But he was travelling on the passport belonging to Giacomo Venturini, one of the men we've been looking for. Also, he was in possession of this.' He places the briefcase on the table, opens it, and hands Cattaneo a bundle of notes. 'If you have them examined, you'll see they're mostly counterfeit.'

The inspector fans the notes out. 'Do they match the one we found in the print shop?'

'I believe they're from the same source.'

'They look used,' says the chief, holding up one of the notes.

'They've been laundered to look that way. According to Caruso, the gang's been recruiting men without records, tricking them with a story that they'll be set up with business prospects on arrival in New York. The men then provided documents necessary to get through Immigration and the money to pay for their passage across the Atlantic.'

'But why would they pay in the first place if they're given a bag full of cash?'

'The victims weren't told about the money. The prospect of a new life was enough. From their side, the money paid was considered a show of faith, a down payment in the business. Caruso says members of the gang, all of whom are out on bail, or on the run, for crimes committed in Sicily, are given passports, other personal documents, and about 1000 dollars, half of which is bad coin.'

'How are they getting away with it on the other side?' asks Cattaneo. 'That kind of money must attract attention?'

'Immigration looks kindly on individuals who aren't looking for a handout and who might be looking to invest in the city. Of course, there is the occasional bribe to smooth over any bumps.'

'So what happened once they paid their dues and handed over their documents?' says Alvise. 'Where are Venturini and the others?'

'After Scalisi leaked the information about our raid, the operation was moved to a location out of town. A farmhouse. A pig farm to be precise. The property belongs to a blood relative of Morello.'

'Do you think they're still alive?' says Alvise.

He breathes heavily. 'If they are, then we need to get to them quickly. If Di Primo and the others know we're coming, they're likely to burn the place down and disappear. But if we move fast, we'll catch them in the act and have enough evidence to shut down a large part of Don Vito's network in Milan. And hopefully squeeze the man himself out from whichever hole he's hiding in.'

'What makes you sure it has anything to do with the Don?' says Cattaneo.

'Because of the Morello connection. He's Don Vito's man in New York.'

'So why not simply snatch Morello?'

'We've tried before.'

'We?' says Alvise.

'I mean, the New York police,' he says, averting his eyes.

The journalist lowers his head and then, as if he has just remembered something, turns towards the darkroom.

'I'm not going to ask you about your interrogation methods, but I don't like any of this,' says the chief. 'How can we trust anything that comes out of this Sicilian Caruso's mouth? With these *mafiosi*, it's either *acqua in bocca*, or they're spitting out lies.'

'Two things,' the detective says, grasping his rotund belly, 'I trust this gut of mine, and Caruso is too stupid to make up a story like this.'

'What do you need from me?'

'If we are going to move in on the farmhouse then we need men you trust.'

'Especially after what happened to the man from Rome,' says the journalist.

'Hold it right there, Inchiostro,' says the inspector, 'Scalisi was an outsider. Sergeant Bruno has been with me a long time, and Esposito came to me fresh out of training college. I can trust them.'

'OK,' says Alvise, 'I'm just saying – '

'I hear what you're saying and I'm telling you I can trust them.'

'You'll do it then?' asks the detective.

The inspector looks him in the eyes. 'I doubted you before, more than once, if I'm honest, but you've been right, and I owe you one.'

The detective nods and pushes the briefcase across the desk. 'I'll leave this with you,' he says. 'I suspect there is some real money where we're going.'

'I need to brief my men first,' says Cattaneo. 'Let's meet back here in an hour, so we can lay out our plan of action.' The inspector picks up the briefcase and leaves.

Nineteen

With Cattaneo gone, Alvise regards the detective with unnerving attentiveness. 'So how did you get this Caruso to talk?' he asks.

'I didn't have to do anything. You saw for yourself where he spent the night and with whom. Not a scratch on the man, though. Whatever they did to him, it was effective. Any leads on Ruiz?'

The journalist pushes himself up from his desk. 'Not much, but there is something. Lock that door.' The detective nods and turns the latch.

Alvise takes a key from his desk drawer and unlocks the darkroom.

'You lock it even when you're here in the office?'

'I'm in and out a lot. I don't take any chances. You think Cattaneo has a rat problem? Well, the newspaper business is a proverbial plague.'

The adjoining darkroom is dimly lit. Photographs hang pegged to lines of thread strung across the room like rows of washlines. Specially made large, rectangular containers are fitted into the surface of a table against the far wall.

The detective looks closely at the drying square sheets of paper. Mostly pictures of men and women at social gatherings. But pinned on the back wall, beneath a unique brass lamp with an amber bulb, close-ups of men are arranged in a grid, much like the detective's own pyramid of *mafiosi* tacked on the back of his door at the *pensione*. A few of the faces are familiar to him: Gianni Gambino, Giovanni Pappalardo, and the wiry Sicilian, Rizzo. All of whom have been struck through with a bold line of black ink.

'You're not going to find Ruiz, not on my wall anyway.'

'Why's that?'

'Because he's careful. There's very little to tell you. His full name is Ismael Martinez Ruiz, but he is known on the street simply as *Lo Spagnolo*, and he is feared, so much so that my informers seemed nervous even mentioning him. He's believed to have honed his killing skills as a Spanish soldier fighting in Cuba before switching to the side of the rebels. Then when the Americans entered the conflict, he apparently became one of the Men of Mamby. He has a reputation for his deadly skill with daggers.'

'I think I know something about that.'

'If it was Ruiz who attacked Madam Xuan, then you're both lucky to be alive.'

'Must have had an off day.'

'Of course, this is all hearsay. What's certain is that he's now a ruthless but professional assassin, and he has definite ties to Don Vito.'

'Do you think the Don's here in Milan?'

'My sources don't seem to think so, and even if he is, then the man is invisible.' Alvise pauses. 'Also,' he continues, with a slight change of tone, 'there's an ongoing investigation that he is implicated in. I did some digging in the archives.'

The detective knows what's coming. He shifts his stance and faces the photographs of the dead.

'I thought there was something familiar about you the day we first met,' says the journalist. 'I couldn't quite place it, but I knew I'd seen you before.' He slaps an old copy of the *Milan Gazette* down in front of the detective. 'March 12, Palermo. Bad day for you?'

'The worst,' he says. He picks up the paper. The article reports his murder at the hands of 'killers unknown' in Piazza Marina. The photograph is an old one of him outside the courthouse in Lower Manhattan, striding proudly up the street beside the prisoner Tommaso Petto. It had been the first day of trial in the notorious Barrel Murder case.

'If it hadn't been for the derby,' says the journalist, 'I may never have put the pieces together. It's not exactly a subtle wardrobe choice, certainly not in this city.'

The detective reaches instinctively for his hat, only to realise that he left it in the other room. With his eyes still averted, he folds the paper and returns it to the journalist.

'I'm guessing the chief already knows. A lot of things make sense now,' says Alvise. 'You should be more careful. It hasn't been that long since….'

The detective fixes his eyes on the photograph of Don Vito, the black felt fedora masking his features. Devil-like in the subdued amber light. 'Maybe you're right,' he says. 'But it seems like forever.'

With the sky threatening to come down, the detective walks briskly along Via Garibaldi. Passing a *profumeria*, he suddenly stops. In the window display, tiny ornate bottles of French perfume lie nestled on plush satin cushions. *Blenheim Bouquet, La Rose Jacqueminot*, and *L'Origan* by *Coty,* Paris. Adelina's favourite. How she would love to be here. He considers going in to buy her a gift, a bottle of *L'Origan*, like he did in the old days just after they were married. They'd not gone on honeymoon. He'd been too busy on a case. And although she understood, he regretted it. More so now that it was too late. Not being a spendthrift, she'd never indulged in things like chocolates, perfumes, or any of the luxuries other men's wives seemed to be preoccupied with. So, when he could afford to, he'd spoilt her, buying her perfume. *L'Origan.*

A young woman stands beside him now, looking at the window display. In the reflection of the glass, he sees that her eyes move from the elegant bottles of perfume to him. And her expression, at first delighted by the display, turns sombre. She lowers her eyes, brushes a lock of hair behind her ear, then hurries away.

He sees himself as if through her eyes. His short, heavyset stature, his long overcoat, and derby perched on his round face. Perhaps he gave others the impression of an English banker, or an undertaker. He wonders what the woman had seen to cause the sudden change in her.

The darkness overhead deepens. Shadows of passers-by rush past in all directions. And before he knows it the heavens break. He holds on to his hat and strides forward into the pelting rain.

In his room, he stands drenched before his reflection in the mirror. The wet clothes feel heavy. He recalls the young woman outside the *profumeria*, and he cannot shake the idea that she'd seen something to distress her.

He turns to his door and stares at the faces of the men responsible for the crimes against his happiness, for that is how he sees them now. They have robbed him of his wife and daughter, of his freedom, his life as he knew it. He rips the derby from his head. Water streaks his face. Had the young woman seen him for who he was? Had she recognised the NYPD detective, gunned down in the street? If she didn't recognise him, she was perhaps reminded of him. The derby hat, the overcoat. He himself has seen his picture in the paper from all those months ago, hailed as a hero, a procession in his honour down the streets of Palermo and New York.

He goes over to the clothes stand in the corner. He slowly removes his long, rain-soaked overcoat and hangs it up, then sets his derby on top. There, now he has stepped out of himself. Once more, he stands in front of the mirror, loosens the collar of his shirt, undoes the buttons. He sees his scars, on his right shoulder, neck, and cheek. He touches his face, feels the rough two-day beard on his pockmarked skin. Still recognizably himself. But no longer Joseph Petrosino.

Twenty

C hief Inspector Cattaneo has picked a small squad of only himself, Sergeant Bruno, and the young officer, Michele Esposito. The detective carries his .38 and Alvise has been given a revolver, a Single Action Colt, the old but reliable Peacemaker. Just before sunrise, the men leave the paddy wagon and ascend the hill.

From behind a low, stone wall, they look down on the farmland half a kilometre away. With a pair of binoculars, the detective scopes out the farmhouse. Di Primo's red Model T Ford is parked out front. They watch and wait. Occasionally, Ismael Ruiz comes out onto the porch to smoke. Otherwise, the house appears unguarded.

They wait for the Spaniard to finish smoking and return inside. Alvise, it is decided, will keep watch in case anyone else should come to the house via the dirt road. Then, with the sun behind them, breaking weakly through the cloud, they begin their advance. The element of surprise is in their favour.

Sergeant Bruno goes first, running down the hill, followed closely by Esposito, who provides him with cover. Positioned behind the Model T, they secure the porch and signal to the detective and the inspector who move in, descending from opposite sides. They do a quick sweep of the perimeter of the house. In the distant penumbra, the detective makes out a fenced enclosure of wooden poles and chicken wire. Pigs grunt, jostling at a trough. Some root around in the mud. The stench causes him to cover his mouth and nose and move off quickly. All the windows at the back of the house are behind closed shutters. There is no view of what's happening inside or how many men they're dealing with, other than the two they know of, Ruiz and Di Primo.

The detective decides to lead into the house. Esposito holds his position behind the automobile, while Bruno and Cattaneo flank the front door. The detective cocks his gun.

Reaching for the doorknob, he hears approaching footsteps, the heavy tread of boots. He signals to the others, then steps beside Cattaneo. As Ruiz walks out onto the porch, the detective presses his gun to the man's head.

'Don't make a sound. Hands behind your head.'

The Spaniard, surprisingly calm for a man with the muzzle of a .38 against his skull, raises his hands. Beneath his bristling moustache, a rolled cigarette dangles from his lips. His eyes hang lazily on the detective.

'Search him,' says the chief inspector. Bruno does a swift pat-down, removing two intricately crafted daggers from inside his cavalry jacket, along with a Beretta Stampede, and a small hunting knife worn on his calf just above the left boot. Ruiz's eyes remain indifferent, fixed all the while on the detective, moving from his face to the slight bulge on his right arm. His moustache twitches, the unlit cigarette bobs up and down like the needle in a gage.

'Now, turn around, slowly,' says the detective.

Cattaneo holds the door open. The Spaniard turns and, urged by the detective's gun, walks back into the house. Though light shines at the end of the passage, the rest of the house is in darkness. While Bruno does a sweep of the other rooms, the detective and the Spaniard, followed by the inspector, walk slowly into the kitchen.

At a small table, the clerk and Di Primo sit, each working beneath his own gas lamp. They look up, and Di Primo makes a move for the *lupara* in the middle of the table, but the inspector is faster, rushing in with his Smith and Wesson trained on Di Primo.

'Bad idea,' says the chief. 'Stand up, both of you, hands behind your heads.' The clerk looks terrified, as usual. Perhaps he was born with the look of terror in his eyes. Di Primo shakes his head, stubs out his cigar, and slowly gets to his feet. He doesn't seem to recognise the detective.

Sergeant Bruno joins them in the kitchen, then he and Cattaneo search the men. Both are unarmed. As the three men's hands are cuffed behind them, the clerk pleads his innocence. Di Primo glares at him in disgust. *'Chiudi il becco, Farini.' Shut your beak.* The detective has seen weak men crack under pressure before, but never in front of the very men who would be there to cut their throats inside a cell.

'You best be quiet now,' he says to the clerk. 'You're not helping any.'

The inspector picks up one of the passports. 'Where are these men?' he asks, looking at Ruiz, who even disarmed possesses an air of danger and authority over the others. He doesn't answer.

'I've checked all the rooms,' says Bruno, 'there's nobody else in the house.'

'Giacomo Venturini and the others,' says the detective, jutting the barrel of his .38 into the base of Ruiz skull, 'what's happened to them?'

Still, Ruiz says nothing. The cigarette remains dangling from his lips. The inspector steps up and rips it from the Spaniard's mouth, throws it to the floor, then crushes it under his heel.

'I don't like the look of you,' he says, getting up in Ruiz's face. The Spaniard grins, baring his yellowed canines, then snaps his teeth, feigning to bite Cattaneo. The inspector scowls and jabs a threatening fist beneath the man's chin. If it were up to the detective, Ruiz would already be spitting blood and teeth. But he knows Cattaneo won't lash out, not in front of Sergeant Bruno.

He notices a chain around Ruiz's neck. On it is a key.

'What's this then?' asks the detective.

Ruiz keeps grinning but says nothing. Again, the detective is tempted to knock the smile off his face. The man's so deep under his skin that he's itching for some violence. He yanks the key, breaking the chain. Ruiz's smile remains, but his eyes darken.

'Right,' says the inspector, 'let's get these men back to the jailhouse.'

'I've done nothing,' says the clerk, his voice breaking.

'*Sta zitto, cazzo*,' hisses Di Primo.

They march the men out onto the porch. Alvise has joined Esposito behind the Model T. Both men seem relieved to see them. Esposito gathers Ruiz's weapons into a sack and the inspector hands him the *lupara*.

'*Bene ragazzi*,' says the chief, 'get this lot back to the wagon and into custody. Separate cells. And you two keep a watch on them personally. The rest of us will stay behind and wait for the forensics. Sergeant Bruno send me Tamanini, that's all.'

'Let's move,' says the sergeant, taking charge of Ruiz, poking his revolver into the Spaniard's back. Passing the Model T, Di Primo glances sadly at the automobile, flinching his shoulder under Esposito's firm hold. The snivelling clerk leads the way unaccompanied, while the other two in check drag their feet. The Spaniard looks back, keeping his eyes on the detective until they are up the hill, where the sun fails to break through the dark clouds camping on the horizon.

'Let's see what we can find,' says Cattaneo. 'Inchiostro, unfortunately there are no bodies today, but I'm sure you can find something of interest, just remember – '

'I know, don't touch anything. I'll have a look around out here.'

Cattaneo nods and goes back into the house followed by the detective. They open the shutters in the lounge and upstairs. Judging by the bookshelf of yellow-band detective stories, and the stack of old newspapers by the fireplace, it seems to be a regular family home. Whoever lived there doesn't seem to be around anymore. Apart from the unmade beds, the bedrooms appear orderly. No signs of *malavita*. No guns lying about, or bottles of liquor. It's certainly no den of thieves.

In the kitchen there is the lingering smell of tobacco and ashtrays piled with the cigar butts smoked by Di Primo. Ruiz must have always smoked outside on the porch, never in the company of the Sicilian.

Beneath the gas lamps remain the unfinished passports which Di Primo and the clerk Farini were in the process of doctoring.

Leading off from the kitchen is a door.

'It's locked,' says the inspector.

'Let's try this.' He passes him the key on the chain.

'That's the one,' says Cattaneo, unlocking the door.

Then, taking up a lamp each, they go down a narrow passage of stairs into the basement.

On the floor are large canvas sacks filled with notes, some folded, some rolled and fastened with rubber bands. The walls are lined with shelves packed with jars of preserves, tin cans, olive oil, and dusty bottles of wine. The back shelf is packed with more money, neatly stacked and separated, half dollar, half lire.

Cattaneo takes up a wad of lire notes and holds it close to the light. 'You think it's real?'

The detective shakes his head. 'I'm guessing it's much the same as the other lot we found.' He kicks at the sack. 'Here's how they achieved that used look.'

Footsteps approach from above. 'Velletri? Chief?' says Alvise anxiously. The detective cocks his .38 and Cattaneo pulls out his revolver. They go cautiously up the stairs. Alvise paces, pulling his cap from his head.

'What's got into you?' asks the inspector, lowering his gun. 'You'd better come outside.'

They follow him round to the back of the house. He stops and points to the pigpen. The detective and Cattaneo exchange worried glances. They proceed tentatively and lean into the enclosure. Some of the pigs lie idle, most of them still root about in the mud. In a gap between their frenzied snouts, a man's hand sticks out from the ground. Two younger pigs feast on an arm.

'*Dio mio.*'

The detective fires a round into the air. While the young pigs scatter, the older ones merely look around before continuing to feast. He covers his mouth with his handkerchief and kicks open the gate to the enclosure. All the pigs scurry off as he approaches, shouting.

Half buried in the mud lies a naked man. The side of his face emerges recognisable. He knows those features from memory. Giacomo Venturini is dead.

In a corner of the pen, in amongst charred wood, strewn pieces of clothing lie beneath pairs of shoes. Alvise stands beside him now, reaching for his camera. He's hands are shaking.

Twenty-one

Ismael Ruiz feels the barrel thrust between his shoulder blades as he's made to descend the hill. An automobile waits on the edge of a backroad. How'd the police find them? Farini hadn't the backbone to be a snitch, yet still he'd kept a close eye on him ever since Gambino's death. He's never trusted men who waste their lives sitting at desks. There must be someone else. Again, the officer jabs him in the back.

'Pick up your feet, soldier,' he says.

Soldier. He knows these failed military men well, men who fail at war only to join the police, settle for a low rank, then spend the rest of their miserable lives pretending it means something. Just like this officer, who now carries his daggers in a sack. He's grateful they weren't left back at the farm, in the hands of that smug bastard who'd tried to trick him. He knew what he was up to the moment he saw him. That scar on the side of his face said it all. Taking him for an idiot, asking after their business and the Model T. He wishes he'd dealt with that *puta madre* when he'd had the chance. He may have failed to hit La Madrina, but at least he'd drawn that man's blood. Next time he'll use Toledo steel, and make sure. And there will be a next time.

'Move it,' says the officer, shoving him forward as they reach the vehicle. Farini and Di Primo already sit waiting in the back of the wagon. What a pair they are. He's ashamed to have fallen with the likes of them. If they'd been real men instead of cowardly Italians, they may have put up a fight, might well still be free men, feeding these lawmen to the pigs. At least Di Primo has the good sense to keep his mouth shut. If Farini isn't snivelling, then he's begging for his life. He's going to have to shut him up one way or another.

'Get on up in there,' says the officer. 'No talking.'

He climbs up the stepladder, ducking his head as he takes a seat in the far end of the wagon opposite the second policeman.

'You got these boys?' says the officer. 'Any trouble, you use your baton, you hear?'

The young officer nods, slipping his baton out from his belt. He carries a police issue revolver in his holster. The senior officer gives him an encouraging look, then shuts the doors. He can be heard cranking the engine. It starts up with a racket. Farini mumbles to himself with his eyes shut, probably praying. Di Primo stares at the poor bastard with contempt. Bet if he had his hands free, he'd strangle him. One thing a Sicilian can't stomach is a snitch.

The road is bumpy, and they bounce about in the back, doing their best not to topple over. He stares at the young officer. Just a dressed-up kid with a gun. He can't be more than 20. Must be doing well for himself to be taken along on this job. Not for the soft hearted. He smiles at *este chico* who averts his gaze. That's it. He's spooked. Ruiz considers his next move carefully. It cannot be more than two or three kilometres before they reach the main road. If he's going to act, it needs to be now. He leans towards the officer, pretends to whisper something, his face concerned, gesturing with his head towards the babbling Farini. The kid buys it.

'What's that?' he says, leaning in, so as to hear better.

Ruiz lunges forward, headbutting the officer clean on the base of his forehead, breaking the kid's nose, and knocking him out.

Farini begins to yell.

'*Sta zitto,*' says Di Primo. '*Idiota.*'

But it's too late. The officer up front has heard the commotion. He slows down and pulls over. Ruiz, quickly on his back, manoeuvres his arms past his legs, to the front of his body, then he grabs the revolver from the kid's holster. As the other officer unlocks the back, the hysterical Farini gets to his feet, presses up against the doors. Di Primo leans back and kicks Farini crashing through the opening doors and out towards the officer who fires a shot, hitting the flailing clerk. The officer struggles out from under Farini's body and is quick to his feet again. But Ruiz is faster and fells him with a shot to the head.

'*Occhio all'altro,*' warns Di Primo.

Ruiz turns in time to see the bloodied face of the kid bearing down on him with a baton. He shoots the young officer with his own gun, hitting him in the heart. He topples dead.

After the gunshot rings out, there is silence.

Ruiz looks down at the dead youngster. He was right, *este chico fue valiente.*

Di Primo laughs nervously. '*Bravo, l'hai fatto,*' he says.

Ruiz snorts and climbs down from the wagon. Out on the dirt road, the bodies lie one on top of the other. He gives a swift kick to the leg of Farini, then the officer. Dead. He finds the keys to the cuffs easy enough in the top pocket of the officer's shirt. He sets the gun down on the man's chest and fishes out the keys. He won't be able to unlock the cuffs himself. He picks up the revolver again.

'*Vieni qui,*' he says to Di Primo.

The Sicilian's legs are shaking, and he practically falls out the wagon.

'*Girarti,*' says Ruiz.

Di Primo looks worried. '*Cosa?*'

Smiling, Ruiz shakes the keys at him. Di Primo relaxes and turns, allowing Ruiz to unlock the cuffs.

'*Ora a me, amigo?*' says Ruiz.

Di Primo looks him in the eyes, then down at the blood splattered on his shirt, at the revolver still in his grip. It doesn't take much to follow the Sicilian's thoughts.

'Don Vito *ci aspetta,*' says Ruiz. The name of the Don has the desired effect.

'*Va bene,*' says Di Primo, taking the keys from him, '*ma prima dammi la pistola.*'

Ruiz clicks his tongue and drops the gun to the ground. '*Niente più colpi.*'

Di Primo hunches down, picks up the gun, and places it in the seat of his trousers. '*Un souvenir,*' he says, half smiling. He unlocks Ruiz's cuffs. He rubs his wrists, working the blood back into circulation.

Di Primo throws the cuffs aside. '*Ora che facciamo?*'

Ruiz steps forward, grabs him by the throat, and pushes him against the wagon. Before the Sicilian can react, Ruiz snatches back the revolver and shoves it under the man's chin. Di Primo looks more confused than afraid.

'*El último*,' says Ruiz. Then he pulls the trigger.

The Sicilian collapses dead in the dust.

Ruiz looks back up towards the rise. They're bound to have heard the shots. He quickly turns Farini's body over, uncuffs him, and plants the revolver in his right hand. Let the police work that one out. The left side of his mouth twitches into a smile, and he twists his moustache.

He goes to the front of the wagon, finds the sack, opens it. He takes back his weapons, kissing his daggers, and Di Primo's *lupara*, which he swings over his shoulder.

Then, Ismael Martinez Ruiz, careful not to leave tracks, scampers off through the mist in the direction of the distant farmlands.

Twenty-two

The inspector opens the gates, and they drive the pigs out. Some of them are stubborn and need prodding before they get up out of the mud. They wander down on their own to a river at the bottom of the valley.

While there was enough to identify Venturini's body, there are four other corpses, half dug up, whose features the pigs have left marred beyond recognition. Their deaths were less recent. There may be others.

Alvise does not speak at all. He takes pictures of the enclosure. For the most part, he stays outside the fence, not wanting to upset any of the evidence. Or fall prey to evil.

Having seen enough, the detective returns to the front of the house. Staring out towards the hills, he chews on a cigar. Cattaneo soon joins him. Like Atlas, bearing the weight of the world, the inspector lowers himself slowly to the porch steps.

'I've worked homicide cases most of my career,' he says, knocking mud from the heels of his shoes. 'I'd say as many as a hundred. But I've never seen such brutality, such a disregard for human life.'

The detective takes the cigar from his mouth and slowly faces the inspector. 'You know it's been grey like this for over a week,' he says.

'You're going to talk about the weather now?'

'You see that heavy cloud over there?' the detective continues. 'I swear it's been following me. Getting darker by the day.'

The inspector stares coldly at him, brushing his hand back over his head.

'That cloud broke yesterday,' he goes on, 'and it'll break again, and it's going to really come down, but afterwards, well, we need to make sure we're the ones still here when it's gone.'

The inspector is silent. He looks past the detective and into the distance. Then he nods and, putting his hands on his knees, pushes himself up.

Gunshots ring out in the distance.

The inspector looks at the detective whose eyes fall on the red automobile.

'Crank up the engine,' he says, throwing his cigar to the ground.

They abandon the Model T at the foot of the rise. At the top of the hill, the three men take cover behind a stone wall. Cattaneo surveys the land below through the binoculars. Judging by the deep furrows on the inspector's forehead, it's bad. The detective can see the road ahead for himself. Under a shifting shroud of low-lying mist, the police wagon waits in the middle of the dirt road.

Cattaneo lowers the binoculars and reaches for his gun. 'Inchiostro, stay here and cover us until I give the all-clear. Velletri, you move in from the left, see those trees down there? It's probably all over, but I don't want to be ambushed. Let's go.'

The detective cocks his .38 and follows the inspector's lead. The closer he gets to the mist, the more he sees. Keeping his eyes on Cattaneo, the cluster of cypress trees to the left, and the paddy wagon, he watches for any kind of movement. To the right, leading off from the road, there is a far-stretching valley of farmlands. The mist gives the nearby cypress trees the appearance of ghostly figures. Only their height distinguishes them from men. A fox darts across his path.

He comes to the cluster of cypresses at the same time the inspector reaches the vehicle. He waits. There is no sound or signal from Cattaneo, so he beelines it across to the front of the wagon. In the driver's seat, there is nothing but the empty sack.

He takes count of the dead. Ruiz is not among them. Di Primo lies in a heap beside the back wheel. The bullet took off the top of his head. An execution kill. His numbered days came to a messy end.

In the back of the wagon, young Esposito lies bent forward in an unnatural position. The baton in his fist stretches ahead of him. Pointing out into the murky distance. A clue perhaps to which way Ruiz has fled.

He joins the chief inspector. With his arms at his sides, clutching his gun in a fierce grip, Cattaneo stands over the body of Sergeant Bruno. 'All clear,' he says, under his breath.

Then he gives into that weight and falls to his knees. He brushes dust from Bruno's forehead and shuts the man's eyes with his thumb.

Beside the dead officer, the clerk lies face up, eyes and mouth gaping at the dark sky, his expression no less fearful in death than it was in life. A police issue .38 is held feebly in his slack grip. Perhaps he found something to fight for in the end. Maybe he chose the right side. Although it doesn't look that way.

The detective raises his hand, signalling to Alvise. The journalist runs down the hill but then stops himself as he nears the scene. Averting his eyes, he walks slowly up to the detective and hands him the Peacemaker.

'I'll wait there,' he says, walking on past him, turning his camera over in his hands. 'I'm out of….'

But his words trail off as he wanders away down the dirt road into the mist. There is no end in sight.

Twenty-three

Outside the city mortuary, he waits for Marianne Greco. He'd warned her about what she'd see, told her she might prefer to live with her memories of her husband as he had been. But she was adamant, said she needed to be sure. And she wanted to go alone.

He scratches at his beard, which he has yet to get used to, and bides his time reading the *Milan Gazette*. The foreign press has condemned the leadership of Antonio Maura in his handling of the conflict in Barcelona which has resulted in more than a hundred civilians dead. The *La Vanguardia* has called it 'la Semana Trágica.' He finds himself saying a prayer for the souls of Sergeant Bruno and young Esposito. For the soul of Hao. Of Giacomo Venturini and all the others.

Marianne leaves the mortuary. She crosses the road with her eyes on her feet. Her steps are slow and hesitant. Prayers will not console the living, nor bring back the dead.

They walk in silence back to Chinatown, towards the *pensione*, where her children are being looked after. She holds her purse in front of her with both hands. He thinks of things he should say, but each time he opens his mouth, the words retreat.

In the end, it is she who speaks. 'You found him. That's something, for now.'

'For now?' he says. 'I wish – '

She stops walking and looks around at the people going about their day. She puts her hand on his chest. 'Find the men who killed my husband, and make them suffer, promise me.'

He nods, bringing his hand to hers. He wants to say the words, say he promises her, but again the words fail him. She slips her hand from beneath his and walks on.

At the *pensione*, the vases in the lobby are once again filled with flowers. The young maids fuss over baby Giona, who giggles as Yang gallops the wooden horse across his little belly. Aurora's laughter reaches them from Xuan's rooms.

There, they sit on the cushions at the low table. Aurora's bear lies tumbled over beside her. The table is covered with small satin flowers which Xuan has taught the child to thread together into bracelets. Aurora sees her mother and runs to her.

'Mamma,' she says, raising her tiny wrist. Then she runs back and chooses another of the bracelets. '*Questo è per te,*' she says, '*l'ho fatto io da sola.*' *This one's for you, I made it myself.*

'*È bellissimo, grazie,*' says her mother, slipping on the bracelet. Then, hugging her daughter, she smiles at Xuan.

'Aurora is very good with her hands,' says Xuan. 'I said she could come and arrange the flowers in my shop one day.'

'*Sì,*' says the child, kneeling again at her workplace.

'In the meantime,' says Xuan, 'I'd like to offer you a job. If you're interested.'

'A job?' Marianne says.

'In my flower shop. I need someone to manage things,' she says. 'I have my hands full here.'

Marianne watches as Aurora carefully begins to thread yet another bracelet.

'That's kind,' she says, 'but I have the children and – '

'The shop is nearby,' Xuan says. 'And Yang will take care of them. Think about it.'

'*Sí, va bene*,' says Aurora, grabbing a handful of flowers.

The detective takes a step back, and then another, until he is at the door.

'Joe,' says Xuan, before he can slip away. 'Your beard, it suits you.'

The women both smile. But the child, gazing up at him suddenly, as if she hadn't noticed him there before, drops the satin flowers and covers her eyes with her small hands.

Acknowledgements

Joe Petrosino by Arrigo Petacco is an authoritative account on the life and tragic death of Lieutenant Joseph Petrosino. It was an invaluable resource. Many thanks to my editorial team: Gwen Joy Uno, Fernando Dantas, Amy Suiter Clarke, Rachel McDonald. And special thanks to Hannes Pasqualini for the cover design on this series. Lastly, thank you to my family for their honest thoughts and encouragement along the way.

About the Author

Ryan Licata was born in Benoni, South Africa. He graduated from the University of Cape Town and later lived in the hills of Trentino, northern Italy. He earned an MFA at Kingston University, receiving the MFA Prize. After attaining his Ph.D. from the University of Edinburgh, he returned to Italy. He currently lives in the town of Caldonazzo.

Ryan's short stories feature in *The Ram Boutique Vol 1,* the Kingston University Press anthologies *Ripple* and *Writings,* and the literary magazine *Storgy.*

Printed in Great Britain
by Amazon

53812805R00090